Burn is great stuff. Smart, funny, formidable, and unlike anything else out there. James Patrick Kelly has written some of my very favorite short stories. As a matter of fact, I get anxious when I haven't read a Kelly story in a while. Can't we just clone him?

— KELLY LINK, HUGO AND NEBULA WINNER, AUTHOR OF
Magic For Beginners

A dynamic tale with brains and heart. Thoreau's ideas on simplicity and civil disobedience rub against one another, and they ignite.

— EILEEN GUNN, NEBULA AWARD WINNING AUTHOR OF
Stable Strategies and Others

James Patrick Kelly is one of the masters of science fiction. He imagines futures both high-tech and human, both dizzyingly complicated and determinedly simple, and then sends us to Walden, where simplicity is anything but, and even Henry David Thoreau begins to look disturbingly different. Burn is inventive, moving, and involving. It's James Patrick Kelly at his best, and there's nothing better.

— CONNIE WILLIS, HUGO AND NEBULA AWARD WINNING
AUTHOR OF *Doomsday Book*

Kelly's special genius is in writing stories that are so human that they wrench and warm your heart at the same moment. Combine that with the kind of vivid, alien techno-extrapolation in *Burn*, and you get a powerful cocktail of the strange and the hauntingly familiar.

— CORY DOCTOROW, AUTHOR OF *Someone Comes to Town,
Someone Leaves Town* AND CO-EDITOR OF BOING BOING

James Patrick Kelly's *Burn*'s deceptively simple surface veils a half-dozen paradoxes. In a distant galactic future, it takes us to a new world that seems old, replete with human comedy and personal tragedy. It tells us about town ball and apples and forest fires. It gives us a world of fully realized human beings in the hands of post-human politics, and a hero and heroine you'll care about, turned round and round by fate or the gods or powers who think they know what is best for them. *Burn* is a story of love, loss, luck, and fate, and you won't forget it.

— JOHN KESSEL, AUTHOR OF *Good News From Outer Space*

Burn may seem at first like a space opera with firefighters and Transcendentalists, but there's more going on beneath its compelling story — questions of progress and responsibility, intervention and witness, technology and truth. The ending is extraordinary, forcing us to reconsider everything we've taken for granted in the story so far. This is science fiction that Thoreau himself might love!

— MATTHEW CHENEY, COLUMNIST, *Strange Horizons*

☼ BURN

Burn

JAMES PATRICK KELLY

TACHYON PUBLICATIONS | SAN FRANCISCO

Cover illustration © 2005 by John Picacio.
Cover design © 2005 by Ann Monn.
Interior design & composition by John D. Berry.
The typeface is Freight Text, with Freight Micro.

Tachyon Publications
1459 18th Street #139
San Francisco, CA 94107
(415) 285-5615
www.tachyonpublications.com

Series Editor: Jacob Weisman

ISBN: 1-892391-27-9

Printed in the United States of America
by the Maple-Vail Book Manufacturing Group

First Edition: 2005

9 8 7 6 5 4 3 2 1

For H. D. T.
a timeless visionary
and
for my children,
Maura, Jamie, and John

✲ *BURN*

☼

We might try our lives by a thousand simple tests; as, for instance, that the same sun which ripens my beans illumines at once a system of earths like ours. If I had remembered this it would have prevented some mistakes. This was not the light in which I hoed them. The stars are the apexes of what wonderful triangles! What distant and different beings in the various mansions of the universe are contemplating the same one at the same moment! Nature and human life are as various as our several constitutions. Who shall say what prospect life offers to another?

    – WALDEN

☼ ONE

For the hero is commonly the simplest and obscurest of men.
— WALDEN

Spur was in the nightmare again. It always began in the burn. The front of the burn took on a liquid quality and oozed like lava toward him. It licked at boulders and scorched the trees in the forest he had sworn to protect. There was nothing he could do to fight it; in the nightmare, he wasn't wearing his splash pack. Or his fireproof field jacket. Fear pinned him against an oak until he could feel the skin on his face start to cook. Then he tore himself away and ran. But now the burn leapt after him, following like a fiery shadow. It chased him through a stand of pine; trees exploded like firecrackers. Sparks bit through his civvies and stung him. He could smell burning hair. His hair. In a panic he dodged into a stream choked with dead fish and poached frogs. But the water scalded his legs. He scrambled up the bank of the stream, weeping. He knew he shouldn't be afraid; he was a veteran of the firefight. Still he felt as if something was squeezing him. A whimpering gosdog bolted across his path, its feathers singed, eyes wide. He could feel the burn dive under the forest and burrow ahead of him in every direction. The ground was hot beneath his feet and the dark humus smoked and stank. In the nightmare there was just one way out, but his brother-in-law Vic was blocking it. Only in the nightmare Vic was a pukpuk, one of the human torches who had started the burn. Vic had not yet set himself on fire, although his baseball jersey was smoking in the heat. He beckoned and for a moment Spur thought it might not be Vic after all as the anguished face shimmered in the heat of the burn. Vic wouldn't betray them, would he? But by then Spur had to dance to keep his shoes from catching fire, and he had no escape, no choice, no time. The torch spread his arms wide and Spur stumbled into his embrace and with an angry whoosh they exploded together into flame. Spur felt his skin crackle....

"That's enough for now." A sharp voice cut through the nightmare. Spur gasped with relief when he realized that there was no burn. Not here anyway. He felt a cold hand brush against his forehead like a blessing and knew that he was in the hospital. He had just been in the sim that the upsiders were using to heal his soul.

"You've got to stop thrashing around like that," said the docbot. "Unless you want me to nail the leads to your head."

Spur opened his eyes but all he could see was mist and shimmer. He tried to answer the docbot but he could barely find his tongue in his own mouth. A brightness to his left gradually resolved into the sunny window of the hospital room. Spur could feel the firm and not unpleasant pressure of the restraints, which bound him to the bed: broad straps across his ankles, thighs, wrists and torso. The docbot peeled the leads off his temples and then lifted Spur's head to get the one at the base of his skull.

"So do you remember your name?" it said.

Spur stretched his head against the pillow, trying to loosen the stiffness in his neck.

"I'm over here, son. This way."

He turned and stared into a glowing blue eye, which strobed briefly.

"Pupil dilatation normal," the docbot muttered, probably not to Spur. It paused for a moment and then spoke again. "So about that name?"

"Spur."

The docbot stroked Spur's palm with its med finger, collecting some of his sweat. It stuck the sample into its mouth. "That may be what your friends call you," it said, "but what I'm asking is the name on your ID."

The words chased each other across the ceiling for a moment before they sank in. Spur wouldn't have had such a problem understanding if the docbot were a person, with lips and a real mouth instead of the oblong intake. The doctor controlling this bot was somewhere else. Dr. Niss was an upsider whom Spur had never actually met. "Prosper Gregory Leung," he said.

"A fine Walden name," said the docbot, and then muttered, "Self ID 27.4 seconds from initial request."

"Is that good?"

It hummed to itself, ignoring his question. "The electrolytes in your sweat have settled down nicely," it said at last. "So tell me about the sim."

"I was in the burn and the fire was after me. All around, Dr. Niss. There was a pukpuk, one of the torches, he grabbed me. I couldn't get away."

"You remembered my name, son." The docbot's top plate glowed with an approving amber light. "So did you die?"

Spur shook his head. "But I was on fire."

"Experience fear vectors unrelated to the burn? Monsters, for instance? Your mom? Dad?"

"No."

"Lost loves? Dead friends? Childhood pets?"

"No." He had a fleeting image of the twisted grimace on Vic's face at that last moment, but how could he tell this upsider that his wife's brother had been a traitor to the Transcendent State? "Nothing." Spur was getting used to lying to Dr. Niss, although he worried what it was doing to his soul.

"Check and double check. It's almost as if I knew what I was doing, eh?" The docbot began releasing the straps that held Spur down. "I'd say your soul is on the mend, Citizen Leung. You'll have some psychic scarring, but if you steer clear of complex moral dilemmas and women, you should be fine." It paused, then snapped its fingers. "Just for the record, son, that was a joke."

"Yes, sir." Spur forced a smile. "Sorry, sir." Was getting the jokes part of the cure? The way this upsider talked at once baffled and fascinated Spur.

"So let's have a look at those burns," said the docbot.

Spur rolled onto his stomach and folded his arms under his chin. The docbot pulled the hospital gown up. Spur could feel its medfinger pricking the dermal grafts that covered most of his back and his buttocks. "Dr. Niss?" said Spur.

"Speak up," said the docbot. "That doesn't hurt does it?"

"No, sir." Spur lifted his head and tried to look back over this shoulder. "But it's really itchy."

"Dermal regeneration 83 percent," it muttered. "Itchy is alive, son. Itchy is growing."

"Sir, I was just wondering, where are you exactly?"

"Right here." The docbot began to flow warm dermslix to the grafts from its medfinger. "Where else would I be?"

Spur chuckled, hoping that was a joke. He could remember a time when he used to tell jokes. "No, I mean your body."

"The shell? Why?" The docbot paused. "You don't really want to be asking about QICs and the cognisphere, do you? The less you know about the upside, the better, son."

Spur felt a prickle of resentment. What stories were upsiders telling each other about Walden? That the citizens of the Transcendent State were backward fanatics who had simplified themselves into savagery? "I wasn't asking about the upside, exactly. I was asking about you. I mean ... you saved me, Dr. Niss." It wasn't at all what Spur had expected to say, although it was certainly true. "If it wasn't for you, it ... I was burnt all over, probably going crazy. And I thought. ..." His throat was suddenly so tight that he could hardly speak. "I wanted to ... you know, thank you."

"Quite unnecessary," said the docbot. "After all, the Chairman is paying me to take care of all of you, bless his pockets." It tugged at Spur's hospital gown with its gripper arm. "I prefer the kind of thanks I can bank, son. Everything else is just used air."

"Yes, but...."

"Yes, but?" It finished pulling the gown back into place. "'Yes but' are dangerous words. Don't forget that you people lead a privileged life here — courtesy of Jack Winter's bounty and your parents' luck."

Spur had never heard anyone call the Chairman Jack. "It was my grandparents who won the lottery, sir," he said. "But yes, I know I'm lucky to live on Walden."

"So why do you want to know what kind of creature would puree his mind into a smear of quantum foam and entangle it with a bot brain a hundred and thirty-some light-years away? Sit up, son."

Spur didn't know what to say. He had imagined that Dr. Niss must be posted nearby, somewhere here at the upsiders' compound at Concord, or perhaps in orbit.

"You do realize that the stars are very far away?"

"We're not simple here, Dr. Niss." He could feel the blood rushing in his cheeks. "We practice simplicity."

"Which complicates things." The docbot twisted off its medfinger and popped it into the sterilizer. "Say you greet your girlfriend on the tell. You have a girlfriend?"

"I'm married," said Spur, although he and Comfort had separated months before he left for the firefight and, now that Vic was dead, he couldn't imagine how they would ever get back together.

"So you're away with your squad and your wife is home in your village mowing the goats or whatever she does with her time. But when you talk on the tell it's like you're sitting next to each other. Where are you then? At home with her? Inside the tell?"

"Of course not."

"For you, of course not. That's why you live on Walden, protected from life on the upside. But where I come from, it's a matter of perspective. I believe I'm right here, even though the shell I'm saved in is elsewhere." The sterilizer twittered. "I'm inhabiting this bot in this room with you." The docbot opened the lid of the sterilizer, retrieved the medfinger with its gripper and pressed it into place on the bulkhead with the other instruments. "We're done here," it said abruptly. "Busy, busy, other souls to heal, don't you know? Which reminds me: We need your bed, son, so we're moving your release date up. You'll be leaving us the day after tomorrow. I'm authorizing a week of rehabilitation before you have to go back to your squad. What's rehab called on this world again?"

"Civic refreshment."

"Right." The docbot parked itself at its station beside the door to the examining room. "Refresh yourself." Its head-plate dimmed and went dark.

Spur slid off the examination table, wriggled out of the

hospital gown and pulled his uniform pants off the hanger in the closet. As he was buttoning his shirt, the docbot lit its eye. "You're welcome, son." Its laugh was like a door slamming. "Took me a moment to understand what you were trying to say. I keep forgetting what it's like to be anchored."

"Anchored?" said Spur.

"Don't be asking so many questions." The docbot tapped its dome. "Not good for the soul." The blue light in its eye winked out.

☆ Two

Most of the luxuries and many of the so-called comforts of life are not only not indispensable, but positive hindrances to the elevation of mankind.
– WALDEN

Spur was in no hurry to be discharged from the hospital, even if it was to go home for a week. He knew all too well what was waiting for him. He'd find his father trying to do the work of two men in his absence. Gandy Joy would bring him communion and then drag him into every parlor in Littleton. He'd be wined and dined and honored and possibly seduced and be acclaimed by all a hero. He didn't feel like a hero and he surely didn't want to be trapped into telling the grandmas and ten-year-old boys stories about the horrors of the firefight.

But what he dreaded most was seeing his estranged wife. It was bad enough that he had let her little brother die after she had made Spur promise to take care of him. Worse yet was that Vic had died a torch. No doubt he had been in secret contact with the pukpuks, had probably passed along information about the Corps of Firefighters — and Spur hadn't suspected a thing. It didn't matter that Vic had pushed him away during their time serving together in Gold Squad — at one time they had been best friends. He should have known; he might have been able to save Vic. Spur had already decided that he would have to lie to Comfort and his neighbors in Littleton about what had happened, just as he had lied to Dr. Niss. What was the point in smearing his dead friend now? And Spur couldn't help the Cooperative root out other pukpuk sympathizers in the Corps; he had no idea who Vic's contacts had been.

However, Spur had other reasons for wanting to stay right where he was. Even though he could scarcely draw breath without violating simplicity, he loved the comforts of the hospital. For example, the temperature never varied from a scandalous twenty-three degrees Celsius. No matter that outdoors the sun was blistering the rooftops of the upsiders' Benevolence Park Number 5, indoors was a paradise where neither sweat nor sweaters held sway. And then there was the food. Even though Spur's father, Capability Roger Leung, was the richest man in Littleton, he had practiced stricter simplicity than most. Spur had grown up on meat, bread, squash and scruff, washed down with cider and applejack pressed from the Leungs' own apples and the occasional root beer. More recently, he and Rosie would indulge themselves when they had the money, but he was still used to gorging on the fruits of the family orchard during harvest and suffering through preserves and root cellar produce the rest of the year. But here the patients enjoyed the abundance of the

Thousand Worlds, prepared in extravagant style. Depending on his appetite, he could order lablabis, dumplings, goulash, salmagundi, soufflés, quiche, phillaje, curry, paella, pasta, mousses, meringues or tarts. And that was just the lunch menu.

But of all the hospital's guilty pleasures, the tell was his favorite. At home Spur could access the latest bazzat bands and town-tunes from all over Walden plus six hundred years of opera. And on a slow Tuesday night, he and Comfort might play one of the simplified chronicles on the tiny screen in Diligence Cottage or watch a spiritual produced by the Institute of Didactic Arts or just read to each other. But the screens of the hospital tells sprawled across entire walls and, despite the Cooperative's censors, opened like windows onto the universe. What mattered to people on other worlds astonished Spur. Their chronicles made him feel ignorant for the first time in his life and their spirituals were so wickedly materialistic that he felt compelled to close the door to his hospital room when he watched them.

The search engine in particular excited Spur. At home, he could greet anyone in the Transcendent State — as long as he knew their number. But the hospital tell could seemingly find anyone, not only on Walden but anywhere on all the Thousand Worlds of the upside. He put the tell in his room to immediate use, beginning by greeting his father and Gandy Joy, who was the village virtuator. Gandy had always understood him so much better than Comfort ever had. He should have greeted Comfort as well, but he didn't.

He did greet his pals in the Gold Squad, who were surprised that he had been able to track them down while they were on active duty. They told him that the entire Ninth Regiment had been pulled back from the Motu River burn for two weeks of CR in Prospect. Word was that they were being reassigned to the Cloyce Memorial Forest for some easy fire watch duty. No doubt the Cooperative was yanking the regiment off the front line because Gold Squad had taken almost 40 percent casualties when the burn had flanked their position at Motu. Iron and Bronze Squads had taken a hit as well, fighting their way through the burn to rescue Gold.

To keep from brooding about Vic and the Motu burn and the firefight, Spur looked up friends who had fallen out of his life. He surprised his cousin Land, who was living in Slide Knot in Southeast and working as a tithe assessor. He connected with his childhood friend Handy, whom he hadn't seen since the Alcazars had moved to Freeport, where Handy's mom was going to teach pastoral philosophy. She was still at the university and Handy was an electrician. He tracked down his self-reliance school sweetheart, Leaf Benkleman, only to discover that she had emigrated from Walden to Kolo in the Alumar system. Their attempt to catch up was frustrating, however, because the Cooperative's censors seemed to buzz every fifth word Leaf said. Also, the look on her face whenever he spoke rattled Spur. Was it pity? He was actually relieved when she cut their conversation short.

Despite the censors, talking to Leaf whetted Spur's appetite for making contact with the upside. He certainly wouldn't get the chance once he left the hospital. He didn't care that everyone was so preposterously far away that he would never meet them in person. Dr. Niss had been wrong: Spur understood perfectly the astonishing distances between stars. What he did not comprehend was exactly how he could chat with someone who lived hundreds of trillions of kilometers away, or how someone could beam themselves from Moy to Walden in a heartbeat. Of course, he had learned the simplified explanation of QICS — quantum information channels — in school. QICS worked because many infinitesimally small nothings were part of a something, which could exist in two places at the same time. This of course made no sense, but then so much of upsider physics made no sense after the censors were done with it.

Spur paused in the doorway of his room and looked up and down the hall. None of the patients at his end of the ward were stirring; a lone maintenance bot dusted along the floor at the far end by the examining rooms. It was his last full day at the hospital. Now or never. He eased the door shut and turned the tell on.

He began by checking for relatives on the upside. But when he searched on the surname Leung, he got 2.3×10^6 hits. Which, if any, of them might be his people? Spur had no way of knowing. Spur's grandparents had expunged all records of their former lives when they had come to Walden, a requirement for immigrants to the Transcendent State. Like everyone else in his family, he had known the stern old folks only as GiGo and GiGa. The names on their death certificates were Jade Fey Leung and Chap Man-Leung, but Spur thought that they had probably been changed when they had first arrived at Freeport.

He was tempted to greet his father and ask if he knew GiGo's upside name, but then he would ask questions. Too many questions; his father was used to getting the answers he wanted. Spur went back to the tell. A refined search showed that millions of Leungs lived on Blimminey, Eridani Foxtrot, Fortunate Child, Moy, and No Turning Back, but there also appeared to be a scattering of Leungs on many of the Thousand Worlds. There was no help for it; Spur began to send greetings at random.

He wasn't sure exactly who he expected to answer, but it certainly wasn't bots. When Chairman Winter had bought Walden from ComExplore IC, he decreed that neither machine intelligences nor enhanced upsiders would be allowed in the refuge he was founding. The Transcendent State was to be the last and best home of the true humans. While the pukpuks used bots to manufacture goods that they sold to the Transcendent State, Spur had never actually seen one until he had arrived at the hospital.

Now he discovered that the upside swarmed with them. Everyone he tried to greet had bot receptionists, secretaries, housekeepers or companions screening their messages. Some were virtual and presented themselves in outlandish sims; others were corporeal and stared at him from the homes or workplaces of their owners. Spur relished these voyeuristic glimpses of life on the upside, but glimpses were all he got. None of the bots wanted to talk to him, no doubt because of the caution he could see scrolling across his screen. It warned that his greeting originated from "the Transcendent State of Walden, a jurisdiction under a consensual cultural quarantine."

Most of bots were polite but firm. No, they couldn't connect him to their owners; yes, they would pass along his greeting; and no, they couldn't say when he might expect a greeting in return. Some were annoyed. They invited him to read his own Covenant and then snapped the connection. A couple of virtual bots were actually rude to him. Among other things, they called him a mud hugger, a leech and a pathetic waste of consciousness. One particularly abusive bot started screaming that he was "a stinking useless fossil."

Spur wasn't quite sure what a fossil was, so he queried the tell. It returned two definitions: 1. an artifact of an organism, typically extinct, that existed in a previous geologic era; 2. something outdated or superseded. The idea that, as a true human, he might be outdated, superseded or possibly even bound for extinction so disturbed Spur that he got up and paced the room. He told himself that this was the price of curiosity. There were sound reasons why the Covenant of Simplicity placed limits on the use of technology. Complexity bred anxiety. The simple life was the good life.

+

Yet even as he wrestled with his conscience, he settled back in front of the tell. On a whim he entered his own name. He got just two results:

> *Comfort Rose Joerly and Prosper Gregory Leung*
> *Orchardists*
> *Diligence Cottage*
> *Jane Powder Street*
> *Littleton, Hamilton County,*
> *Northeast Territory, TS*
> *Walden*
> *and*
> *Prosper Gregory Leung*
> *c/o Niss (remotely — see note)*
> *Salvation Hospital*
> *Benevolence Park #5*
> *Concord, Jefferson County,*
> *Southwest Territory, TS*
> *Walden*

Spur tried to access the note attached to Dr. Niss's name, but it was blocked. That wasn't a surprise. What was odd was that he had received results just from Walden. Was he really the only Prosper Gregory Leung in the known universe?

While he was trying to decide whether being unique was good or bad, the tell inquired if he might have meant to search for Proper Gregory Leung or Phosphor Gregory L'ung or Procter Gregoire Lyon? He hadn't but there was no reason not to look them up. Proper Leung, it turned out, raised gos-dogs for meat on a ranch out in Hopedale, which was in the

Southwest Territory. Spur thought that eating gosdogs was barbaric and he had no interest in chatting with the rancher. Gregory L'ung lived on Kenning in the Theta Persei system. On an impulse, Spur sent his greeting. As he expected, it was immediately diverted to a bot. L'ung's virtual companion was a shining green turtle resting on a rock in a muddy river.

"The High Gregory of Kenning regrets that he is otherwise occupied at the moment," it said, raising its shell up off the rock. It stood on four human feet. "I note with interest that your greeting originates from a jurisdiction under a consensual...."

The turtle didn't get the chance to finish. The screen shimmered and went dark. A moment later, it lit up again with the image of a boy, perched at the edge of an elaborate chair.

He was wearing a purple fabric wrap that covered the lower part of his body from waist to ankles. He was bare-chested except for the skin of some elongated, dun-colored animal draped around his thin shoulders. Spur couldn't have said for sure how old the boy was, but despite an assured bearing and intelligent yellow eyes, he seemed not yet a man. The chair caught Spur's eye again: it looked to be of some dark wood, although much of it was gilded. Each of the legs ended in a stylized human foot. The back panel rose high above the boy's head and was carved with leaves and branches that bore translucent purple fruit.

That sparkled like jewels.

Spur reminded himself to breathe. It looked very much like a throne.

☆ Three

It takes two to speak the truth — one to speak and another to hear.

– A WEEK ON THE CONCORD AND MERRIMACK RIVERS

"Hello, hello," said the boy. "Who is doing his talk, please?"

Spur struggled to keep his voice from squeaking. "My name is Prosper Gregory Leung."

The boy frowned and pointed at the bottom of the screen. "Walden, it tells? I have less than any idea of Walden."

"It's a planct."

"And tells that it's wrongful to think too hard on planet Walden? Why? Is your brain dry?"

"I think." Spur was taken aback. "We all think." Even though he thought he was being insulted, Spur didn't want to snap the connection — not yet anyway. "I'm sorry, I didn't get your name."

The words coming out of the speakers did not seem to match what the boy was saying. His lips barely moved, yet what Spur heard was, "I'm the High Gregory, Phosphorescence of Kenning, energized by the Tortoise of Eternal Radiation." Spur realized that the boy was probably speaking another language and that what he was hearing was a translation. Spur had been expecting the censors built into the tell to buzz this conversation like they had buzzed so much of his chat with Leaf Benkleman, but maybe bad translation was just as effective.

"That's interesting," said Spur cautiously. "And what is it that you do there on Kenning?"

"Do?" The High Gregory rubbed his nose absently. "Oh, do! I make luck."

"Really? People can do that on the upside?"

"What is the upside?"

"Space, you know." Spur waved an arm over his head and glanced upward.

The High Gregory frowned. "Prosper Gregory Leung breathes space?"

"No, I breathe air." He realized that the tell might easily be garbling his end of the conversation as well. "Only air." He spoke slowly and with exaggerated precision. "We call the Thousand Worlds the upside. Here. On my world."

The High Gregory still appeared to be confused.

"On this planet." He gestured at the hospital room. "Planet Walden. We look up at the stars." He raised his hand to his brow, as if sighting on some distant landmark. "At night." Listening to himself babble, Spur was certain that the High Gregory must think him an idiot. He had to change the subject, so he tapped his chest. "My friends call me Spur."

The High Gregory shook his head with a rueful smile. "You give me warmth, Spur, but I turn away with regret from the kind offer to enjoy sex with you. Memsen watches to see that I don't tickle life until I have enough of age."

Aghast, Spur sputtered that he had made no such offer, but the High Gregory, appearing not to hear, continued to speak.

"You have a fullness of age, friend Spur. Have you found a job of work on planet Walden?"

"You're asking what I do for a living?"

"All on planet Walden are living, I hope. Not saved?"

"Yes, we are." Spur grimaced. He rose from the tell and retrieved his wallet from the nightstand beside the bed. Maybe pix would help. He flipped through a handful in his wallet until he came to the one of Comfort on a ladder picking apples. "Normally I tend my orchards." He held the pix up to the tell to show the High Gregory. "I grow many kinds of fruit on my farm. Apples, peaches, apricots, pears, cherries. Do you have these kinds of fruit on Kenning?"

"Grape trees, yes." The High Gregory leaned forward in his throne and smiled. "And all of apples: apple pie and apple squeeze and melt apples." He seemed pleased that they had finally understood one another. "But you are not normal?"

"No. I mean yes, I'm fine." He closed the wallet and pocketed it. "But ... how do I say this? There is fighting on my world." Spur had no idea how to explain the complicated grievances of the pukpuks and the fanaticism that led some of them to burn themselves alive to stop the spread of the forest and the Transcendent State. "There are other people on Walden who are very angry. They don't want my people to live here. They wish the land could be returned to how it was before we came. So they set fires to hurt us. Many of us have been called to stop them. Now instead of growing my trees, I help to put fires out."

"Very angry?" The High Gregory rose from his throne, his face flushed. "Fighting?" He punched at the air. "Hit-hit-hit?"

"Not exactly fighting with fists," said Spur. "More like a war."

The High Gregory took three quick steps toward the tell at his end. His face loomed large on Spur's screen. "War fighting?" He was clearly agitated; his cheeks flushed and the yellow eyes were fierce. "Making death to the other?" Spur had no idea why the High Gregory was reacting this way. He didn't think the boy was angry exactly, but then neither of them had proved particularly adept at reading the other. He certainly didn't want to cause some interstellar incident.

"I've said something wrong. I'm sorry." Spur bent his head in apology. "I'm speaking to you from a hospital. I was wounded . . . fighting a fire. Haven't quite been myself lately." He gave the High Gregory a self-deprecating smile. "I hope I haven't given offense."

The High Gregory made no reply. Instead he swept from his throne, down a short flight of steps into what Spur could now see was a vast hall. The boy strode past rows of carved wooden chairs, each of them a unique marvel, although none was quite as exquisite as the throne that they faced. The intricate beaded mosaic on the floor depicted turtles in jade and chartreuse and olive. Phosphorescent sculptures stretched like spider webs from the upper reaches of the walls to the barrel-vaulted ceiling, casting ghostly silver-green traceries of light on empty chairs beneath. The High Gregory was muttering as he passed down the central aisle but whatever he was saying clearly overwhelmed the tell's limited capacity. All Spur heard was, "War <crackle> Memsen witness there <crackle> our luck <crackle> <crackle> call the L'ung...."

At that, Spur found himself looking once again at a shining green turtle resting on a rock on a muddy river. "The High Gregory of Kenning regrets that he is otherwise occupied at the moment," it said. "I note with interest that your greeting originates from a jurisdiction under a consensual cultural quarantine. You should understand that it is unlikely that the High Gregory, as luck maker of the L'ung, would risk violating your covenants by having any communication with you."

"Except I just got done talking to him," said Spur.

"I doubt that very much." The turtle drew itself up on four human feet and stared coldly through the screen at him. "This conversation is concluded," it said. "I would ask that you not annoy us again."

"Wait, I—" said Spur, but he was talking to a dead screen.

☆ Four

But if we stay at home and mind our business, who will want
railroads? We do not ride on the railroad; it rides upon us.
— WALDEN

Spur spent the rest of that day expecting trouble. He had
no doubt that he'd be summoned into Dr. Niss's examining
room for a lecture about how his body couldn't heal if his soul
was sick. Or some virtuator from Concord would be brought
in to light communion and deliver a reproachful sermon on
the true meaning of simplicity. Or Cary Millisap, his squad
leader, would call from Prospect and scorch him for shirking
his duty to Gold, which was, after all, to get better as fast he
could and rejoin the unit. He had not been sent to hospital to
bother the High Gregory of Kenning, luck maker of the L'ung
— whoever they were.

But trouble never arrived. He stayed as far away from his
room and the tell as he could get. He played cards with Val
Montilly and Sleepy Thorn from the Sixth Engineers, who
were recovering from smoke inhalation they had suffered
in the Coldstep burn. They were undergoing alveolar recon-

struction to restore full lung function. Their voices were like ripsaws but they were otherwise in good spirits. Spur won enough from Sleepy on a single round of Fool All to pay for the new apple press he'd been wanting for the orchard. Of course, he would never be able to tell his father or Comfort where the money had come from.

Spur savored a memorable last supper: an onion tart with a balsamic reduction, steamed duck leg with a fig dressing on silver thread noodles and a vanilla panna cotta. After dinner he went with several other patients to hear a professor from Alcott University explain why citizens who sympathized with the pukpuks were misguided. When he finally returned to his room, there was a lone greeting in his queue. A bored dispatcher from the Cooperative informed him that he needed to pick up his train ticket at Celena Station before 11 A.M. No video of this citizen appeared on the screen; all he'd left was a scratchy audio message like one Spur might get on his home tell. Spur took this as a reminder that his holiday from simplicity would end the moment he left the hospital.

The breeze that blew through the open windows of the train was hot, providing little relief for the passengers in the first-class compartment. Spur shifted uncomfortably on his seat, his uniform shirt stuck to his back. He glanced away from the blur of trees racing past his window. He hated sitting in seats that faced backward; they either gave him motion sickness or a stiff neck. And if he thought about it — which he couldn't help but doing, least for a moment — the metaphor always depressed him. He didn't want to be looking back at his life just now.

A backward seat — but it was in first class. The Cooperative's dispatcher probably thought he was doing him a favor. Give him some extra legroom, a softer seat. And why not? Hadn't he survived the infamous Motu River burn? Hadn't he been badly scorched in the line of duty? Of course he should ride in first class. If only the windows opened wider.

It had been easy not to worry about his problems while he was lounging around the hospital. Now that he was headed back home, life had begun to push him again. He knew he should try to stop thinking, maybe take a nap. He closed his eyes, but didn't sleep. Without warning he was back in the nightmare sim again ... and could smell burning hair. His hair. In a panic he dodged into a stream choked with dead fish and poached frogs. But the water was practically boiling and scalded his legs ... only Spur wasn't completely in the nightmare because he knew he was also sitting on a comfortable seat in a first-class compartment in a train that was taking him ... the only way out was blocked by a torch, who stood waiting for Spur. Vic had not yet set himself on fire, although his baseball jersey was smoking in the heat ... I'm not afraid, Spur told himself, I don't believe any of this ... the anguished face shimmered in the heat of the burn and then Spur was dancing to keep his shoes from catching fire, and he had no escape, no choice, no time ... with his eyes shut, Spur heard the clatter of the steel wheels on the track as: no time no time no time no time.

He knew then for certain what he had only feared: Dr. Niss had not healed his soul. How could he, when Spur had consistently lied about what had happened in the burn? Spur didn't mean to groan, but he did. When he opened his eyes, the gandy in the blue flowered dress was staring at him.

"Are you all right?" She looked to be in her late sixties or maybe seventy, with silver hair so thin that he could see the freckles on her scalp.

"Yes, fine," Spur said. "I just thought of something."

"Something you forgot?" She nodded. "Oh, I'm always remembering things just like that. Especially on trains." She had a burbling laugh, like stream running over smooth stones. "I was supposed to have lunch with my friend Connie day after tomorrow, but here I am on my way to Little Bend for a week. I have a new grandson."

"That's nice," Spur said absently. There was one other passenger in the compartment. He was a very fat, moist man looking at a comic book about gosdogs playing baseball; whenever he turned a page, he took a snuffling breath.

"I see by your uniform that you're one of our firefighters," said the gandy. "Do you know my nephew Frank Kaspar? I think he is with the Third Engineers."

Spur explained that there were over eleven thousand volunteers in the Corps of Firefighters and that if her nephew was an engineer he was most probably a regular with the Home Guard. Spur couldn't keep track of all the brigades and platoons in the volunteer Corps, much less in the professional Guard. He said that he was just a lowly smokechaser in Gold Squad, Ninth Regiment. His squad worked with the Eighth Engineers, who supplied transportation and field construction support. He told her that these fine men and women were the very models of spiritual simplicity and civic rectitude, no doubt like her nephew. Spur was hoping that this was what she wanted to hear and that she would leave him alone. But then she asked if the rumors of pukpuk collaborators infiltrating the Corps were true and started nattering about how she couldn't understand how a citizen of the Transcendent State could betray the Covenant by helping terrorists. All the pukpuks wanted was to torch Chairman Winter's forests, wasn't that awful? Spur realized that he would have to play to her sympathy. He coughed and said he had been wounded in a burn and was just out of hospital and then coughed again.

"If you don't mind," he said, crinkling his brow as if he were fighting pain, "I'm feeling a little woozy. I'm just going to shut my eyes again and try to rest."

Although he didn't sleep, neither was he fully awake. But the nightmare did not return. Instead he drifted through clouds of dreamy remembrance and unfocussed regret. So he didn't notice that the train was slowing down until the hiss of the air brakes startled him to full alertness.

He glanced at his watch. They were still an hour out of Heart's Wall, where Spur would change for the local to Littleton.

"Are we stopping?" Spur asked.

"Wheelwright fireground." The fat man pulled a limp handkerchief out of his shirt pocket and dabbed at his hairline. "Five minutes of mandatory respect."

Now Spur noticed that the underbrush had been cleared along the track and that there were scorch marks on most of the trees. Spur had studied the Wheelwright in training. The forest north of the village of Wheelwright had been one of the first to be attacked by the torches. It was estimated that there must have been at least twenty of them, given the scope of the damage. The Wheelwright burn was also the first in which a firefighter died, although the torches never targeted citizens, only trees. The fires they started were always well away from villages and towns; that's why they were so hard to fight. But the Wheelwright had been whipped by strong winds until it cut the trunk line between Concord and Heart's Wall for almost two weeks. The Cooperative had begun recruiting for the Corps shortly after.

As the squealing brakes slowed the train to a crawl, the view out of Spur's window changed radically. Here the forest had yet to revive from the ravages of fire. Blackened skeletons of trees pointed at the sky and the charred floor of the forest baked under the sun. The sun seemed cruelly bright without the canopy of leaves to provide shade. In every direction, all Spur could see was the nightmarish devastation he had seen all too often. No plant grew, no bird sang. There were no ants or needlebugs or wild gosdogs. Then he noticed something odd: the bitter burnt-coffee scent of fresh fireground. And he could taste the ash, like shredded paper on his tongue. That made no sense; the Wheelwright was over three years old.

When the train finally stopped, Spur was facing one of the many monuments built along the tracks to honor fallen firefighters. A grouping of three huge statues set on a pad of stone cast their bronze gazes on him. Two of the firefighters were standing; one leaned heavily on the other. A third had dropped to one knee, from exhaustion perhaps. All still carried their gear, but the kneeling figure was about to shed her splash pack and one of the standing figures was using his jacksmith as a crutch. Although the sculptor had chosen to depict them in the hour of their doom, their implacable metal faces revealed neither distress nor regret. The fearsome simplicity of their courage chilled Spur. He was certain that he wasn't of their quality.

The engine blew its whistle in tribute to the dead: three long blasts and three short. The gandy stirred and stretched. "Wheelwright?" she muttered.

"Yeah," said the fat man.

She started to yawn but caught herself and peered out the open window. "Who's that?" she said, pointing.

A man in a blue flair suit was walking along the tracks, peering up at the passenger cars. He looked very hot and not very happy. His face was as flushed as a peach and his blond hair was plastered to his forehead. Every few meters he paused, cupped his hands to his mouth and called, "Leung? Prosper Gregory Leung?"

FIVE

Fire is without doubt an advantage on the whole. It sweeps and ventilates the forest floor and makes it clear and clean. I have often remarked with how much more comfort & pleasure I could walk in wood through which a fire had been run the previous year. It is inspiriting to walk amid the fresh green sprouts of grass and shrubbery pushing upward through the charred surface with more vigorous growth.

– JOURNAL, 1850

The man waited impatiently as Spur descended from the train, kit slung over his shoulder. Although he did not turn back to look, Spur knew every passenger on the train was watching them. Was he in trouble? The man's expression gave away nothing more than annoyance. He looked to be younger than Spur, possibly in his late twenties. He had a pinched face and a nose as stubby as a radish. He was wearing a prissy white shirt buttoned to the neck. There were dark circles under the armpits of his flair jacket.

"Prosper Gregory Leung of Littleton, Hamilton County, Northeast?" The man pulled a slip of paper from his pocket and read from it. "You are currently on medical leave from the Ninth Regiment, Corps of Firefighters, and were issued a first-class ticket on this day—"

"I know who I am." Spur felt as if a needlebug were caught in his throat. "What is this about? Who are you?"

He introduced himself as Constant Ngonda, a deputy with the Cooperative's Office of Diplomacy. When they shook hands, he noticed that Ngonda's palm was soft and sweaty. Spur could guess why he had been pulled off the train, but he decided to act surprised.

"What does the Office of Diplomacy want with me?"

Just then the engineer blew three short blasts and couplings of the train clattered and jerked as, one by one, they took the weight of the passenger cars. With the groan of metal on metal, the train pulled away from the Wheelwright Memorial.

Spur's grip on the strap of his kit tightened. "Don't we want to get back on?"

Constant Ngonda shrugged. "I was never aboard."

The answer made no sense to Spur, who tensed as he calculated his chances of sprinting to catch the train. Ngonda rested a hand on his arm.

"We go this way, Prosper." He nodded west, away from the tracks.

"I don't understand." Spur's chances of making the train were fading as it gained momentum. "What's out there?"

"A clearing. A hover full of upsiders." He sighed. "Some important people have come a long way to see you." He pushed a lock of damp hair off his forehead. "The sooner we start, the sooner we get out of this heat." He let go of Spur and started picking his way across the fireground.

Spur glanced over his shoulder one last time at the departing train. He felt as if his life were pulling away.

"Upsiders? From where?"

Ngonda held up an open hand to calm him. "Some questions will be answered soon enough. Others it's better not to ask."

"What do you mean, better?"

Ngonda walked with an awkward gait, as if he expected the ground to give way beneath him. "I beg your pardon." He was wearing the wrong shoes for crossing rough terrain. "I misspoke." They were thin-soled, low-cut and had no laces —little more than slippers. "I meant simpler, not better."

Just then Spur got a particularly intense whiff of something that was acrid and sooty, but not quite smoke. It was what he had first smelled as the train had pulled into the Memorial. He turned in a complete circle, all senses heightened, trying to pinpoint the source. After fire ran through the litter of leaves and twigs that covered the forest floor, it often sank into the duff, the layer of decomposing organic matter that lay just above the soil level. Since duff was like a sponge, most of the year it was too wet to burn. But in the heat of summer it could dry out and became tinder. Spur had seen a smoldering fire burrow through the layer of duff and emerge dozens of meters away. He sniffed, following his nose to a charred stump.

"Prosper!" said Ngonda. "What are you doing?"

Spur heard a soft hiss as he crouched beside the stump. It wasn't any fire sound that he knew, but he instinctively ran his bare hand across the stump, feeling for hotspots. Something cool and wet sprayed onto his fingers and he jerked them back as if he had been burned. He rubbed a smutty liquid between thumb and forefinger and then smelled it.

It had an evil, manmade odor of extinguished fire. Spur sat back on his heels, puzzled. Why would anyone want to mimic that particular stink? Then he realized that his hand was clean when it ought to have been smudged with soot from the stump. He rubbed hard against the burned wood, but the black refused to come off. He could see now that the stump had a clear finish, as if it had been coated with a preservative.

Spur could sense Ngonda's shadow loom over him but then he heard the hissing again and was able to pick out the tiny nozzle embedded in the stump. He pressed his finger to it and the noise stopped. Then on an impulse, he sank his hand into the burned forest litter, lifted it and let the coarse mixture sift slowly through his fingers.

"It's hot out, Prosper," Ngonda said. "Do you really need to be playing in the dirt?"

The litter looked real enough: charred and broken twigs, clumps of leaf mold, wood cinders and a delicate ruined hemlock cone. But it didn't feel right. He squeezed a scrap of burnt bark, expecting it to crumble. Instead it compacted into an irregular pellet, like day-old bread. When he released it, the pellet slowly resumed its original shape.

"It's not real," said Spur. "None of it."

"It's a memorial, Prosper." The deputy offered Spur a hand and pulled him to his feet. "People need to remember." He bent over to brush at the fake pine needles stuck to Spur's knees. "We need to go."

Spur had never seen a hover so close. Before the burns, hovers had been banned altogether from the Transcendent State. But after the pukpuks had begun their terrorist campaign to halt the spread of forest into their barrens, Chairman Winter had given the Cooperative permission to relax the ban. Generous people from the upside had donated money to build the benevolence parks and provided hovers to assist the Corps in fighting fires. However, Chairman Winter had insisted that only bots were to fly the hovers and that citizen access to them would be closely monitored.

While in the field with Gold Squad, Spur had watched hovers swoop overhead, spraying loads of fire-retardant splash onto burns. And he had studied them for hours through the windows of the hospital, parked in front of their hangars at Benevolence Park Number 5. But even though this one was almost as big as Diligence Cottage and hovered a couple of meters above the ground, it wasn't quite as impressive as Spur had imagined it.

He decided that this must be because it was so thoroughly camouflaged. The hover's smooth skin had taken on the discoloration of the fireground, an ugly mottle of gray and brown and black. It looked like the shell of an enormous clam. The hover was elliptical, about five meters tall in front sweeping backward to a tapered edge, but otherwise featureless. If it had windows or doors, Spur couldn't make them out.

As they approached, the hover rose several meters. They passed into its shadow and Ngonda looked up expectantly. A hatch opened on the underside. A ramp extended to the ground below with a high-pitched warble like birdsong, and a man appeared at the hatch. He was hard to see against the light of the interior of the hover; all Spur could tell for sure was that he was very tall and very skinny. Not someone he would expect to bump into on Jane Powder Street in Littleton. The man turned to speak to someone just inside the hatch. That's when Spur realized his mistake.

"No," she said, her voice airy and sweet. "We need to speak to him first."

As she teetered down the ramp, Spur could tell immediately that she was not from Walden. It was the calculation with which she carried herself, as if each step were a risk, although one she was disposed to take. She wore loose-fitting pants of a sheer fabric that might have been spun from clouds. Over them was a blue sleeveless dress that hung to mid-thigh. Her upper arms were decorated with flourishes of phosphorescent body paint and she wore silver and copper rings on each of her fingers.

"You're the Prosper Gregory of Walden?"

She had full lips and midnight hair and her skin was smooth and dark as a plum. She was a head taller than he was and half his weight. He was speechless until Ngonda nudged him.

"Yes."

"We're Memsen."

✪ Six

*It requires nothing less than a chivalric feeling to sustain
a conversation with a lady.*
  – JOURNAL, 1851

Although it was cooler in the shade of the hover, Spur was far from comfortable. He couldn't help thinking of what would happen if the engine failed. He would have felt more confident if the hover had been making some kind of noise; the silent, preternatural effortlessness of the ship unnerved him. Meanwhile, he was fast realizing that Memsen had not wanted to meet him in order to make friends.

"Let's understand one another," she said. "We're here very much against our will. You should know, that by summoning us to this place, you've put the political stability of dozens of worlds at risk. We very much regret that the High Gregory has decided to follow his luck to this place."

She was an upsider so Spur had no idea how to read her. The set of her shoulders flustered him, as did the way her knees bent as she stooped to his level. She showed him too many teeth and it was clear that she wasn't smiling. And why did she pinch the air? With a great effort Spur tore his gaze away from her and looked to Ngonda to see if he knew what she was talking about. The deputy gave him nothing.

"I'm not sure that I summoned the High Gregory, exactly," Spur said. "I did talk to him."

"About your war."

Constant Ngonda looked nervous. "Allworthy Memsen, I'm sure that Prosper didn't understand the implications of contacting you. The Transcendent State is under a cultural —"

"We grant that you have your shabby deniability." She redirected her displeasure toward the deputy. "Nevertheless, we suspect that your government instructed this person to contact the High Gregory, knowing that he'd come. There's more going on here than you care to say, isn't there?"

"Excuse me," said Spur, "but this really was an accident." Both Memsen and Ngonda stared at him as if he had corncobs stuck in his ears. "What happened was that I searched on my name but couldn't find anyone but me and then the tell at the hospital suggested the High Gregory as an alternative because our names are so similar." He spoke rapidly, worried that they'd start talking again before he could explain everything. "So I sent him a greeting. It was totally random — I didn't know who he was, I swear it. And I wasn't really expecting to make contact, since I'd been talking to bots all morning and not one was willing to connect me. In fact, your bot was about to cut me off when he came on the tell. The High Gregory, I mean."

"So." Memsen clicked the rings on her fingers together.

"He mentioned none of this to us."

"He probably didn't know." Spur edged just a centimeter away from her toward the sunlight. The more he thought about it, the more he really wanted to get out from under the hover.

Ngonda spoke with calm assurance. "There, you see that Prosper's so-called request is based on nothing more than coincidence and misunderstanding." He batted at a fat orange needlebug that was buzzing his head. "The Cooperative regrets that you have come all this way to no good purpose."

Memsen reared suddenly to her full height and gazed down on the two of them. "There are no coincidences," she said, "only destiny. The High Gregory makes the luck he was meant to have. He's here, and he has brought the L'ung to serve as witnesses. Our reason for being on this world has yet to be discovered." She closed her eyes for several moments. While she considered Spur's story she made a low, repetitive plosive sound: pa-pa-pa-ptt. "But this is deeper than we first suspected," she mused.

Spur caught a glimpse of a head peeking out of the hatch above him. It ducked back into the hover immediately.

"So," Memsen said at last, "let's choose to believe you, Prosper Gregory of Walden." She eyed him briefly; whatever she saw in his face seemed to satisfy her. "You'll have to show us the way from here. Your way. The High Gregory's luck has chosen you to lead us until we see for ourselves the direction in which we must go."

"Lead you? Where?"

"Wherever you're going."

"But I'm just on my way home. To Littleton."

She clicked her rings. "So."

"I beg your pardon, Allworthy Memsen," said Ngonda, tugging at the collar of his shirt, "but you must realize that's impossible under our Covenant. . . ."

"It is the nature of luck to sidestep the impossible," she said. "We speak for the High Gregory when we express our confidence that you'll find a way."

She had so mastered the idiom of command that Spur wasn't sure whether this was a threat or a promise. Either way, it gave Ngonda pause.

"Allworthy, I'd like nothing better than to accommodate you in this," he said. "Walden is perhaps the least of the Thousand Worlds, but even here we've heard of your efforts to help preserve the one true species." A bead of sweat dribbled down his forehead. "But my instructions are to accommodate your requests within reason. Within reason, Allworthy. It is not reasonable to land a hover in the commons of a village like Littleton. You must understand that these are country people."

She pointed at Spur. "Here is one of your country people."

"Memsen!" shouted a voice from the top of the ramp. "Memsen, I am so bored. Either bring him up right now or I'm coming down."

Her tongue flicked to the corner of her mouth. "You

wouldn't like it," she called back, "it's very hot." Which was definitely true, although as far as Spur could tell, the weather had no effect on her. "There are bugs."

"That's it!" The High Gregory of Kenning, Phosphorescence of the Eternal Radiation and luck maker of the L'ung, scampered down the ramp of the hover.

"There," he said, "I did it, so now don't tell me to go back." He was wearing green sneakers with black socks, khaki shorts and a T-shirt with a pix of a dancing turtle, which had a human head. "Spur! You look sadder than you did before." He had knobby knees and fair skin and curly brown hair. If he had been born in Littleton, Spur would've guessed that he was ten years old. "Did something bad happen to you? Say something. Do you still talk funny like you did on the tell?"

Spur had a hundred questions but he was so surprised that all he could manage was, "Why are you doing this?"

"Why?" The boy's yellow eyes opened wide. "Why, why, why?" He stooped to pick up a handful of the blackened litter and examined it with interest, shifting it around on his open palm. "Because I got one of my luck feelings when we were talking. They're not like ideas or dreams or anything so I can't explain them very well. They're just special. Memsen says they're not like the feelings that other people get, but that it's all right to have them and I guess it is." He twirled in a tight circle then, flinging the debris in a wide scatter. "And that's why." He rubbed his hands on the front of his shorts and approached Spur. "Am I supposed to shake hands or kiss you? I can't remember."

Ngonda stepped between Spur and the High Gregory as if to protect him. "The custom is to shake hands."

"But I shook with you already." He tugged at Ngonda's sleeve to move him aside. "You have hardly any luck left, friend Constant. I'm afraid it's all pretty much decided with you." When the deputy failed to give way, the High Gregory dropped to all fours and scooted through his legs. "Hello, Spur," said the boy as he scrambled to his feet. The High Gregory held out his hand and Spur took it.

Spur was at once aware that he was sweaty from the heat of the day, while the boy's hand was cool as river rock. He could feel the difference in their size: the High Gregory's entire hand fit in his palm and weighed practically nothing.

"Friend Spur, you have more than enough luck," the boy murmured, low enough so that only Spur could hear. "I can see we're going to have an adventure."

"Stay up there," cried Memsen. "No!" She was glowering up the ramp at the hatch, which had inexplicably filled with kids who were shouting at her. Spur couldn't tell which of them said what.

"When do we get our turn?"

"You let the Greg off."

"We came all this way."

"He's bored? I'm more bored."

"Hey move, you're in my way!"

"But I want to see too."

Several in the back started to chant. "Not fair, not fair!"

Memsen ground her toes into the fake forest floor. "We

have to go now," she said. "If we let them off the hover, it'll take hours to round them up."

"I'll talk to them." High Gregory bounded up the ramp, making sweeping motions with his hands. "Back, get back, this isn't it." The kids fell silent. "We're not there yet. We're just stopping to pick someone up." He paused halfway up and turned to the adults. "Spur is coming, right?"

Ngonda was blotting sweat from around his eyes with a handkerchief. "If he chooses." He snapped it with a quick flick of the wrist and then stuffed it into his pocket, deliberately avoiding eye contact with Spur.

Spur could feel his heart pounding. He'd wanted to fly ever since he'd realized that it was possible and didn't care if simplicity counseled otherwise. But he wasn't sure he wanted to be responsible for bringing all these upsiders to Littleton.

"So." Memsen must have mistaken his hesitation for fear. "You have never been in a hover, Prosper Gregory of Walden?"

"Call him Spur," said the High Gregory. "It doesn't mean you have to have sex with him."

Memsen bowed to Spur. "He has not yet invited us to take that familiarity."

"Yes, please call me Spur." He tried not to think about having sex with Memsen. "And yes," he picked up his kit, "I'll come with you."

"Lead then." She indicated that he should be first up the ramp. Ngonda followed him. Memsen came last, climbing slowly with her small and painstakingly accurate steps.

As he approached the top of the ramp, the coolness of the hover's interior washed over him. It was like wading into Mercy's Creek. He could see that the kids had gathered around the High Gregory. There were about a dozen of them in a bay that was about six by ten meters. Boxes and containers were strapped to the far bulkhead.

"Now where are we going?"

"When do we get to see the fire?"

"Hey, who's that?"

Most of the kids turned to see him step onto the deck. Although well lit, the inside of the hover was not as bright as it had been outside. Spur blinked as his eyes adjusted to the difference.

"This is Spur," said the High Gregory. "We're going to visit his village. It's called Littleton."

"Why? Are they little there?"

A girl of six or perhaps seven sidled over to him. "What's in your bag?" She was wearing a dress of straw-colored brocade that hung down to her silk slippers. The gold chain around her neck had a pendant in the shape of a stylized human eye. Spur decided that it must be some kind of costume.

He slung his kit off his shoulder and set it down in front of her so she could see. "Just my stuff."

"It's not very big," she said doubtfully. "Do you have something in there for me?"

"Your Grace," said Memsen, putting a hand on the girl's shoulder, "we are going to leave Spur alone for now." She turned the girl around and gave her a polite nudge toward the other kids. "You'll have to forgive them," she said to Spur. "They're used to getting their own way."

☼ SEVEN

I have a deep sympathy with war, it so apes the gait and bearing of the soul.
  – JOURNAL, 1840

Spur had studied geography in school and knew how big Walden was, but for the first time in his life he *felt* it. From the ground, the rampant forests restricted what anyone could see of the world. Even the fields and the lakes were hemmed in by trees. Spur had never been to the Modilon Ocean but he'd stood on the shores of Great Kamit Lake. The sky over the lake was impressive, but there was no way to take the measure of its scale. Spur had hiked the Tarata Mountains, but they were forested to their summits and the only views were from ledges. There was a tower on Samson Kokoda that afforded a 360-degree view, but the summit was just 1,300 meters tall.

Now the hover was cruising through the clouds at an altitude of 5,700 meters, according to the tell on the bulkhead. Walden spread beneath him in all its breathtaking immensity. Maps, measured in inflexible kilometers and flat hectares, were a sham compared to this. Every citizen should see what he was seeing, and if it violated simplicity, he didn't care.

Constant Ngonda, on the other hand, was not enjoying the view. He curled on a bench facing away from the hull, which Memsen had made transparent when she'd partitioned a private space for them. His neck muscles were rigid and he complained from time to time about trouble with his ears. Whenever the hover shivered as it contended with the wind, he took a huge gulping breath. In a raspy voice, the deputy asked Spur to stop commenting on the scenery. Spur was not surprised when Ngonda lurched to his feet and tore through the bubble-like bulkhead in search of a bathroom. The wall popped back into place, throwing a scatter of rainbows across its shivering surface.

Spur kept his face pressed to the hull. He'd expected the surface to be smooth and cold, like glass. Instead, it was warm and yielding, as if it were the flesh of some living creature. Below him the lakes and rivers gleamed in the afternoon sun like the shards of a broken mirror. The muddy Kalibobo River veered away to the west as the hover flew into the foothills of the Tarata Range. As the land rolled beneath him, Spur could spot areas where the bright-green hardwood forest was yielding ground to the blue-green of the conifers: hemlock and pine and spruce. There were only a few farms and isolated villages in the shadow of the mountains. They would have to fly over the Taratas to get to Littleton on the eastern slope.

At first Spur had difficulty identifying the familiar peaks.

He was coming at them from the wrong direction and at altitude. But once he picked out the clenched fist of Woitape, he could count forward and back down the range: Taurika, Bootless Lowa and Boroko, curving to the northwest, Kaivuna and Samson Kokoda commanding the plain to the south. He murmured the names aloud, as long as the deputy wasn't around to hear. He had always liked how round the pukpuk sounds were, how they rolled in his mouth. When he'd been trapped in the burn with Vic, he was certain that he would never say them again.

When Chairman Winter bought Morobe's Pea from ComExplore IC, he had thought to rename everything on the planet and make a fresh start for his great experiment in preserving unenhanced humanity. But then a surprising number of ComExplore employees turned down his generous relocation offer; they wanted to stay on. Almost all of these pukpuks could trace their ancestry back to some ancient who had made planetfall on the first colonizing ships. More than a few claimed to be descended from Old Morobe herself. As a gesture of respect, the Chairman agreed to keep pukpuk names for some landforms. So there were still rivers, valleys, mountains and islands, which honored the legacy of the first settlers.

Chairman Winter had never made a secret of his plans for Walden. At staggering personal expense, he had intended to transform the exhausted lands of Morobe's Pea. In their place he would make a paradise that re-created the heritage ecology of the home world. He would invite only true humans to come to Walden. All he asked was that his colonists forsake the technologies, which were spinning out of control on the Thousand Worlds. Those who agreed to live by the Covenant of Simplicity would be given land and citizenship. Eventually both the forest and the Transcendent State would overspread all of Walden.

But the pukpuks had other plans. They wouldn't leave and they refused to give up their banned technologies. At first trade between the two cultures of Walden flourished. In fact, the pukpuk industrial and commercial base propped up the fledgling Transcendent State. Citizens needed pukpuk goods, even if bots manufactured them. As time passed however, the Cooperative recognized that pukpuks' continued presence was undermining the very foundations of the Transcendent State. When the Cooperative attempted to close off the borders in order to encourage local industry, black markets sprang up in the cities. Many citizens came to question the tenets of simplicity. The weak were tempted by forbidden knowledge. For the first time since the founding, the emigration rate edged into the double digits. When it was clear that the only way to save the Transcendent State was to push the pukpuks off the planet, Chairman Winter had authorized the planting of genetically enhanced trees. But once the forest began to encroach on the pukpuk barrens, the burns began.

The pukpuks were the clear aggressors in the firefight; even their sympathizers among the citizenry agreed on that. What no one could agree on was how to accommodate them without compromising. In fact, many of the more belligerent citizens held that the ultimate responsibility for the troubles lay with the Chairman himself. They questioned his decision not to force all of the pukpuks to emigrate after the purchase of Morobe's Pea. And some wondered why he could not order them to be rounded up and deported even now. It was, after all, his planet.

"We've come up with a compromise," said Ngonda as he pushed through the bulkhead into the compartment. He was still as pale as a root cellar mushroom, but he seemed steadier. He even glanced briefly down at the eastern slope of Bootless Lowa Mountain before cutting his eyes away. "I think we can let the High Gregory visit under your supervision."

Memsen, the High Gregory, and a young girl followed him, which caused the bulkhead to burst altogether. Spur caught a glimpse of a knot of kids peering at him before the wall reformed itself two meters farther into the interior of the hover, creating the necessary extra space to fit them all. The High Gregory was carrying a tray of pastries, which he set on the table he caused to form out of the deck.

"Hello, Spur," he said. "How do you like flying? Your friend got sick but Memsen helped him. This is Penny."

"The Pendragon Chromlis Furcifer," said Memsen.

She and Spur studied each other. A little taller but perhaps a little younger than the High Gregory, the girl was dressed hood to boot in clothes made of supple metallic-green scales. The scales of her gloves were as fine as snakeskin while those that formed her tunic looked more like cherry leaves, even to the serrated edges. A rigid hood protected the back of her head. A tangle of thick, black hair wreathed her face.

"Penny," said the High Gregory, "you're supposed to shake his hand."

"I know," she said, but then clasped both hands behind her back and stared at the deck.

"Your right goes to his right." The High Gregory held out his own hand to demonstrate. "She's just a little shy," he said.

Spur crouched and held out his hand. She took it solemnly. They shook. Spur let her go. The girl's hand went behind her back again.

"You have a pretty name, Pendragon," said Spur.

"That's her title." Memsen faced left and then right before she sat on the bench next to Ngonda. "It means war chief."

"Really. And have you been to war, Penny?"

She shook her head—more of a twitch of embarrassment than a shake.

"This is her first," said the High Gregory. "But she's L'ung. She's just here to watch."

"I'm sorry," said Spur. "Who are the L'ung?"

Ngonda cleared his throat in an obvious warning. The High Gregory saw Memsen pinch the air and whatever he'd been about to say died on his lips. The silence stretched long enough for Penny to realize that there was some difficulty about answering Spur's question.

"What, is he stupid?" She scrutinized Spur with renewed interest. "Are you stupid, Spur?"

"I don't think so." It was his turn to be embarrassed. "But maybe some people think that I am."

"This is complicated," said Memsen, filling yet another awkward pause. "We understand that people here seek to avoid complication." She considered. "Let's just say that the L'ung are companions to the High Gregory. They like to watch him make luck, you might say. Think of them as students. They've been sent from many different worlds, for many different reasons. Complications again. There is a political aspect..."

Ngonda wriggled in protest.

"... which the deputy assures us you would only find confusing. So." She patted the bench. "Sit, Pendragon."

The Pendragon collected a macaroon from the pastry tray and obediently settled beside Memsen, then leaned to whisper in her ear.

"Yes," said Memsen, "we'll ask about the war."

Ngonda rose then, but caught himself against a bulkhead as if the change from sitting to standing had left him dizzy. "This isn't fair," he said. "The Cooperative has made a complete disclosure of the situation here, both to Kenning and to the Forum of the Thousand Worlds."

"What you sent was dull, dull, dull, friend Constant," said the High Gregory. "I don't think the people who made the report went anywhere near a burn. Someone told somebody else, and that somebody told them." Just then the hover bucked and the deputy almost toppled onto Memsen's lap. "You gave us a bunch of contracts and maps and pix of dead trees," continued the High Gregory. "I can't make luck out of charts. But Spur was there, he can tell us. He was almost burned up."

"Not about Motu River," said Spur quickly. "Nothing about that." Suddenly everyone was staring at him.

"Maybe," began Ngonda but the hover shuddered again and he slapped a hand hard against the bulkhead to steady himself. "Maybe we should tell him what we've agreed on."

Spur sensed that Memsen was judging him, and that she was not impressed. "If you want to talk in general about fighting fires," he said, "that's different."

Ngonda looked miserable. "Can't we spare this brave man...?"

"Deputy Ngonda," said Memsen.

"What?" His voice was very small.

The High Gregory lifted the tray from the table and offered it to him. "Have a cookie."

Ngonda shrank from the pastries as if they might bite him. "Go ahead then," he said. "Scratch this foolish itch of yours. We can't stop you. We're just a bunch of throwbacks from a nothing world and you're — "

"Deputy Ngonda!" Memsen's voice was sharp.

He caught his breath. "You're Memsen the Twenty-Second and he's the High Gregory of Kenning and I'm not feeling very well." Ngonda turned to Spur, muttering. "Remember, they don't really care what happens to you. Or any of us."

"That's not true," said the High Gregory. "Not true at all."

But Ngonda had already subsided onto his bench, queasy and unvoiced.

"So." Memsen clicked her rings together. "You fight fires."

"I'm just a smokechaser." Ngonda's outburst troubled Spur. He didn't know anything about these upsiders, after all. Were they really any different than pukpuks? "I volunteered for the Corps about a year ago, finished training last winter, was assigned the Ninth Regiment, Gold Squad. We mostly build handlines along the edges of burns to contain them." He leaned against the hull with his back to the view. "The idea is that we scrape off everything that can catch fire, dig to mineral soil. If we can fit a plow or tractor in, then we do, but in rough terrain we work by hand. That's about it. Boring as those reports you read."

"I don't understand." The High Gregory sprawled on the deck, picking idly at his sneakers. "If you're so busy digging, when do you put the fires out?"

"Fire needs three things," he said, "oxygen, fuel and temperature. They call it the triangle of combustion. Think of a burn as a chain of triangles. The sides of every triangle have to connect." He formed a triangle by pressing his thumbs and forefingers together. "Hot enough connects to enough air connects to enough stuff to burn. Take away a side and you break the triangle...." He separated his thumbs. "...and weaken the chain. When a burn blows up, there's no good way to cut off its oxygen or lower the core temperature, so you have to attack the fuel side of the triangle. If you do your job, eventually there's nothing left to burn."

"Then you don't actually put fires out?" The High Gregory sounded disappointed.

"We do, but that's just hotspotting. Once we establish a handline, we have to defend it. So we walk the lines, checking for fires that start from flying sparks or underground runners. Trees might fall across a line. If we find a hotspot, we dig it out with a jacksmith or spray it cold with retardant from our splash packs." He noticed that the Pendragon was whispering again to Memsen. "I'm sorry," he said. "Is there something?"

Memsen gave him a polite smile — at least he hoped it was polite. "She asks about the people who set fire to themselves. Have you ever seen one?"

"A torch?" Spur frowned. "No." The lie slipped out with practiced ease.

"They must be very brave." The High Gregory wriggled across the deck on hands and knees to Spur's kit. "Hey, your bag got burnt here." He held the kit up to the afternoon light pouring through the hull, examining it. "And here too. Do you hate them?"

"No."

"But they tried to kill you."

"Not me. They're trying to kill the forest, maybe the Transcendent State, but not me. They have no idea who I am." He motioned for the kit and the High Gregory dragged it across the compartment to him. "And I don't know any of them. We're all strangers." He opened the kit, rummaged inside and pulled out a pix of Gold Squad. "Here's my squad. That's full firefighting gear we're wearing." Dead friends grinned at him from the pix. Vic, kneeling in the front row of the picture, and Hardy, who was standing next to Spur. He flipped the pix over and passed it to the High Gregory.

"Why are the torches doing this?" said Memsen. "You must have wondered about it. Help us understand."

"It's complicated." He waited for Ngonda to pipe up with the official line, but the deputy was gazing through the hull of the hover with eyes of glass. "They should have gone long ago," said Spur. "They're upsiders, really. They don't belong here anymore."

"A thousand worlds for the new," said Memsen, "one for the true. That's what your chairman says, isn't it?"

"Your parents came here from other worlds," said the High Gregory. "So that's why you think the pukpuks should've been willing to pack up and go. But would you come back with us to Kenning if Jack Winter said you should?"

"That's not why I....." Spur rubbed at his forehead. "I don't know, maybe it is. Anyway, they were my grandparents, not my parents."

The High Gregory slid across the deck and handed the pix of Gold Squad to Memsen. The Pendragon craned her neck to see.

"You have to understand," said Spur, "that the pukpuks hate the new forests because they spread so fast. The trees grow like weeds, not like the ones in my orchard." He glanced over his shoulder at the hills beneath him. They were on the east side of the Taratas now and flying lower. Almost home. "When Walden was still the Pea, this continent was dry and mostly open. The Niah was prairie. There was supposedly this huge desert, the Nev, or the Neb, where Concord is now. The pukpuks hunted billigags and tamed the gosdog herds. Their bots dug huge pits to mine carbonatites and rare earths. Eventually they killed off the herds, plowed the prairies under and exhausted all the surface deposits. They created the barrens, raped this planet and then most of them just left. Morobe's Pea was a dying world, that's why the Chairman picked it. There was nothing for the pukpuks here, no reason to stay until we came."

As the hover swooped low over the treetops, Spur could feel the tug of home as real as gravity. After all he had been through, Littleton was still drowsing at the base of Lamana Ridge, waiting for him. He imagined sleeping in his own bed that night.

"Soon there won't be any more barrens," he said, "just forest. And that will be the end of it."

The High Gregory stared at him with his unnerving yellow eyes. "They're just trying to protect their way of life. And now you're telling them that your way is better."

"No." Spur bit his lip; the truth of what the High Gregory said had long since pricked his soul. "But their way of life is to destroy our way."

Memsen flicked a finger against the pix of Gold Squad.

"And so that's why they started this war?"

"Is this a war?" Spur took the pix from her and tucked it into his kit without looking at it again. "They set fires, we put them out. It's dangerous work, either way."

"People die," whispered the Pendragon.

"Yes," said Spur. "They do."

✡ EIGHT

I have lived some thirty-odd years on this planet, and I have yet to hear the first syllable of valuable or even earnest advice from my seniors.
– JOURNAL, 1852

Spur perched on a stump wondering how to sneak over to the Littleton train station. From where he sat, it looked hopeless. He had just bushwhacked through the forest from the edge of Spot Pond, where the hover had lingered long enough to put him onto the mucky shore. Now he was on the trail that led down Lamana Ridge. Just ahead of him was Blue Valley Road, a rough track that connected a handful of farms to Civic Route 22. CR22 became Broad Street as it passed through Littleton Commons, the village center. If he skulked down Blue Valley, he could hitch a ride on 22. Except who would be out this time of day? Neighbors. Littleton was a small town; his father had no doubt told everyone that his son the hero was due in on the 8:16 train from Heart's Wall. Of course, he could avoid 22 altogether and skirt around town to the train station. Except it was a good ten kilometers between the stump and the station and he was bone tired.

He decided to sit a little longer.

At least Ngonda had kept most of the upsiders out of Littleton. He could imagine Penny and Kai Thousandfold and little Senator-for-Life Dowm spreading through his bewildered village to gawk at family pix and open closets and ask awkward questions. The High Gregory was all Spur had to worry about. He would be stepping off the hover ramp tomorrow morning at Spot Pond with the deputy. He would pose as Ngonda's nephew and the deputy would be Spur's comrade-in-arms from Iron Squad. The High Gregory would spend the day touring Littleton and making whatever luck he could. He would sleep at Spur's house and the day after tomorrow he and Ngonda would catch the 7:57 southbound.

"Spur?" called a familiar voice from up the trail. "Is that Prosper Leung?"

Spur wanted to blurt, "No, not me, not at all." He wanted to run away. Instead he said, "Hello, Sly." There were worse citizens he could have run into than Sly Sawatdee.

The big man lumbered down the path. He was wearing cut-off shorts, one leg of which was several centimeters longer than the other. His barrel belly stretched his shirt, which was unbuttoned to his navel. His floppy hat was two-toned: dirty and dirtier. He was carrying a basket filled with gooseberries. His smile was bright as noon.

"That is my Prosper, I swear. My lucky little pinecone, all safe. But you're supposed to be away at the fires. How did you get here, so far from nowhere?"

"Fell out of the sky."

Sly giggled like a little boy. "Go around that again." Sly was gray as an oak and almost as old as Spur's father, but his years had never seemed a burden to him. If the Transcendent State truly wanted its citizens simple, then Sly Sawatdee was the most civic-minded person in Hamilton County. "You're joking me, no?"

"All right then, I walked."

"Walked from where?"

Spur pointed west.

Sly turned, as if he expected to see that a highway had been miraculously cut through the forest. "Nothing that way but trees and then mountains and then a hell of a lot more trees. That's a truckload of walking, green log. You must be tired. Have a gooseberry?" He offered Spur the basket. When Sly harvested the wild fruit, he just broke whole canes off, instead of picking individual berries. Close work he left to his grandnephews at home.

"All right then," said Spur. "I'm not here. I'm on the train from Heart's Wall. I get in at 8:16."

"Yeah? Then who am I talking to, my own shaggy self? Watch the thorns."

Spur popped one of the striped pink berries into his mouth. It was still warm from the sun; his teeth crunched the tiny seeds. "You don't like any of my answers?" He slung his kit over his shoulder.

"I'll nibble almost anything, Spur, but I spit out what doesn't taste good." He pressed a stubby forefinger into Spur's chest. "Your Sly can tell when you're carrying a secret, happy old shoe. Ease the weight of it off your back and maybe I can help you with it."

"Let's walk." Spur set off down the trail. Ahead the trees parted for Blue Valley Road. "How's my father?"

"Well enough for an old man." Sly fell into step alongside him. "Which is to say not so much of what he was. Said you got burnt when Vic Joerly and those other poor boys got killed." He peered at Spur. "You don't look much burnt."

"I was in a hospital in Concord." They had reached Blue Valley Road, which was nothing more than a couple of dirt ruts separated by a scraggle of weeds. "An upsider doctor saved my life." Spur headed toward CR22. "They can do things you wouldn't believe."

"I'll believe it this very minute if you say so." His mouth twisted like he'd bit into a wormy apple. "Only I never had much use for upsiders."

"Why? Have you ever met one?"

"Not me, but my DiDa used to say how they poke holes in their own brains and cut arms and legs off to sew on parts of bots in their place. Now where's the sense in a good man turning bot?"

There was no arguing with Sly when he got to remembering things his long-suffering father had told him. "I'm guessing you buried Vic already?"

"His body came on the train last Wednesday. The funeral was Friday. Most the village was there, biggest communion in years and just about the saddest day."

"How's Comfort?"

"Hard to say." He grimaced. "I paid respects, didn't chit-chat. But I heard around that she's digging herself quite a hole. Wouldn't take much for her to fall in." He turned away from Spur and picked a stone up off the road. "What about you two?"

"I don't want to talk about it."

"Yeah." He lobbed the stone into the woods. "That's what I heard."

They were coming up on the Bandaran farmstead, corn stalks nodding in the field nearest the road. Spur could hear the wooden clunk of their windmill turning on the whispered breath of the afternoon. It was bringing water up from a well to splash into a dug pond where ducks gabbled and cropped. He tried to keep Sly between himself and the house as they passed, but whether he was noticed or not, nobody called out to him.

The next farmstead belonged to the Sawatdees, where Sly lived with his nephew Sunny and his family. On an impulse, Spur said, "There is a secret."

"Yeah, I know. I'm old, but I still hear the mosquitoes buzz."

"The thing is, I'm going to need your help. And you can't tell anyone."

Sly stepped in front of Spur and blocked his way. "Does anyone know who sat on Gandy Star's cherry pie? The one that she baked for your DiDa?"

Spur grinned. "I hope not."

He prodded Spur in the chest with his finger. "Did they

ever figure the boy who was with Leaf Benkleman the day she got drunk on the applejack and threw up at the Solstice Day picnic?"

"It wasn't me." Spur put a hand on Sly's finger and pushed it away. "I was with you fishing that afternoon."

"Yeah, the fish story." He stood aside and motioned for Spur to pass. "Remember who told that one? The old citizen you always forget to come visit now that you're all grown up." They continued down the road. The Sawatdee farmstead was just around the next bend.

"I remember, Sly. Can you help? I need a ride home right now."

"The cottage or your DiDa's house?"

"Diligence Cottage."

He nodded. "Sunny can take you in the truck."

"No, it has to be you. You're going to be the only one who knows I'm back. Part of the secret."

Sly swung the basket of gooseberries in wider arcs as he walked. "Sunny doesn't want me driving at night anymore."

"Don't worry, you'll be back in plenty of time for supper. But then I'll need you again in the morning. Come get me first thing. I'm meeting someone up at Spot Pond."

"Spot Pond? Nobody there but frogs."

Spur leaned closer to Sly. "I can tell you, but you have to promise to help, no matter what." He lowered his voice. "This is a big secret, Sly."

"How big?" Sly looked worried. "Bigger than a barn?"

"Bigger than the whole village." Spur knew Sly would be pleased and flattered to be the only one in Littleton whom Spur had invited into his conspiracy. "In or out, my friend?"

"In up to here." Sly raised a hand over his head. "Ears open, mouth shut." He giggled.

"Good." Spur didn't give him time to reconsider. "An upsider is coming to visit Littleton."

"An upsider." Sly took this for another joke. "And he parks his spaceship where? On Broad Street?"

"A hover is going to put him off near Spot Pond. He's going to stay with me for a day. One day. Nobody is supposed to know he's from the upside."

"A hover." Sly glanced over one shoulder and then the other, as if he expected to spot the hover following them. "One of those birdbots in our sky."

Spur nodded.

"And you want this?"

The question caught him off guard, because he realized that sometime in the last few hours he had changed his mind. "I do, Sly." Spur wanted to spend more time with the High Gregory and it was fine with him if they were together at Diligence Cottage. He just didn't want to inflict the upsider on the rest of his sleepy village. They wouldn't understand.

Except Sly was shaking his head. "Nothing good ever came of getting tangled up with space people."

"I'm just curious is all," said Spur.

"Curious can't sit still, young sprout. Curious always goes

for the closer look." For the first time since Spur had known him, Sly Sawatdee looked his age. "And now I'm thinking what will happen to your DiDa when you leave us. He's a good man, you know. I've known him all my life."

✧ Nine

For when man migrates, he carries with him not only his birds,
quadrupeds, insects, vegetables and his very sward, but his
orchard also.
– WILD APPLES, 1862

Capability Roger Leung loved apples. He was fond of the
other pomes as well, especially pears and quince. Stone fruits
he didn't much care for, although he tolerated sour cherries
in memory of GiGa's pies. But apples were Cape's favorite,
the ancient fruit of the home world. He claimed that apples
graced the tables of all of Earth's great civilizations: Roman,
Islamic, American and Dalamist. Some people in Littleton
thought that Spur's father loved his apple trees more than he
loved his family. Probably Spur's mother, Lucy Bliss Leung,
had been one of these. Probably that was why she left him
when Spur was three, first to move to Heart's Wall and then
clear across the continent to Providence. Spur never got the
chance to ask her because he never saw her again after she
moved to Southwest. The citizens of Walden did not travel
for mere pleasure.

Spur's grandparents had arrived on Walden penniless

and with only a basic knowledge of farming. Yet hard work and brutal frugality had built their farmstead into a success. However, the price they paid for single-minded dedication to farming was high; of their three children, only Cape chose to stay on the farm as an adult. And even he moved out of Diligence Cottage when he was sixteen and put up a hut for himself at the farthest edge of the Leung property. He was trying to escape their disapproval. Whenever he looked at the tell or visited friends or climbed a tree to read a book, GiGo or GiGa would carp at him for being frivolous or lazy. They couldn't see the sense of volunteering for the fire department or playing left base for the Littleton Eagles when there were chores to be done. Sometimes weeks might pass without Cape saying an unnecessary word to his parents.

Yet it had been Cape who transformed the family fortunes with his apples. When he was eighteen, he began attending classes at the hortischool extension in Longwalk, very much against GiGo's wishes. He had paid tuition out of money earned doing odd jobs around the village — another pointless diversion from home chores that irritated his parents. Cape had become interested in fruit trees after brown rot spoiled almost the entire crop of Littleton's sour cherries the year before. All the farmers in the village raised fruit, but their orchards were usually no more than a dozen trees, all of traditional heirloom varieties. Crops were small, usually just enough for home use because of the ravages of pests and disease. Farmers battled Terran immigrants like tarnished plant bugs, sawflies, wooly aphids, coddling moths, leafrollers, lesser apple worms, and the arch enemy: plum curculio. There were mildews, rusts, rots, cankers, blotches and blights to contend with as well. The long growing season of fruit trees made them vulnerable to successive attacks. Citizens across the Transcendent State debated whether or not Chairman Winter had introduced insect evil and fungal disease into his new Garden of Eden on purpose. The question had never been settled. But at hortischool, Cape learned about neem spray, extracted from the chinaberry tree and the organic insecticide pyrethrum, which was made from dried daisies. And he heard about an amazing cider apple called Huang's Nectar, a disease-resistant early bloomer, well-suited to the climate of Southeast but not yet proven hardy in the north. As much to spite his father as to test the new variety, he had drained his savings and bought a dozen saplings on w4 semi-dwarfing rootstock. He started his own orchard on land he had cleared near his hut. Two years later, he brought in his first—admittedly light—harvest, which nevertheless yielded the sweetest cider and smoothest applejack anyone in Littleton had ever tasted. Cape purchased a handscrew press in his third year and switched from fermenting his cider in glass carboys to huge oak barrels by his fifth. And he bought more apple trees — he never seemed to have enough: McIntosh, GoRed, Jay's Pippin, Alumar Gold, Adam and Eve. Soon he began to grow rootstock and sell trees to other farmers. By the time Cape married Spur's mother, the Leungs were renting land from farmsteads on either side of their original holding. GiGo and GiGa lived long enough to see their son become the most prosperous farmer in Littleton. GiGo, however, never forgave himself for being wrong, or Cape for being right, about the apples.

Cape had given Spur and Comfort his parents' house as a wedding present; Diligence Cottage had been empty ever since GiGa had died. Cape had long since transformed his own little hut into one of the grandest homes in Littleton. Spur had Sly drop him off just down Jane Powder Street from the cottage, hoping to avoid the big house and the inevitable interrogation by his father for as long as possible. After seeing Sly's dismay at the news of the High Gregory's visit, he was thinking he might try to keep the High Gregory's identity from Cape, if he could.

However, as Spur approached the front door, he spotted Cape's scooter parked by the barn and then Cape himself reaching from a ladder into the scaffold branches of one of GiGo's ancient Macoun apples. He was thinning the fruit set. This was twice a surprise: first, because Cape usually avoided the house where he had grown up, and second, because he had been set against trying to rejuvenate the Leungs' original orchard, arguing that it was a waste of Spur's time. In fact the peaches and the plum tree had proved beyond saving. However, through drastic pruning, Spur had managed to bring three Macouns and one Sunset apple, and a Northstar cherry back into production again.

"DiDa!" Spur called out so that he wouldn't startle his father. "It's me."

"Prosper?" Cape did not look down as he twisted an unripe apple free. "You're here already. Something's wrong?" He dropped the cull to the pack of gosdogs waiting below. A female leapt and caught the apple in midair in its long beak. It chomped twice and swallowed. Then it chased its scaly tale in delight, while the others hooted at Cape.

"Everything's fine. There was a last minute change and I managed to get a ride home." Spur doubted his father would be satisfied with this vague explanation, but it was worth a try. "What are you doing up there?" He dropped his kit on the front step of the farmhouse and trudged over to the orchard. "I thought you hated GiGo's useless old trees."

Cape sniffed. "Macoun is a decent enough apple; they're just too damn much work. And since you weren't around to tend to them — but I should come down. You're home, Prosper. Wait, I'll come down."

"No, finish what you're doing. How are things here?"

"It was a dry spring." He culled another green apple, careful to grasp the fruiting spur with one hand and the fruit with the other. "June was parched too, but the county won't call it a drought yet." The gosdogs swirled and tumbled beneath him as he let the apple fall. "The June drop was light, so I've had to do a lot of thinning. We had sawfly but the curculio isn't so bad. They let you out of the hospital so soon, Prosper? Tell me what you're not telling me."

"I'm fine. Ready to build fence and buck firewood."

"Have you seen Comfort yet?"

"No."

"You were supposed to arrive by train."

"I hitched a ride with a friend."

"From Concord?"

"I got off the train in Wheelwright."

"Wheelwright." One of the gosdogs was trying to scrabble up the ladder. "I don't know where that is exactly. Somewhere in Southeast, I think. Lee County maybe?"

"Around there. What's wrong with Macouns?"

"Ah." He shook his head in disapproval. "A foolish tree that doesn't know what's good for it." He gestured at the immature apples all around him. "Look at the size of this fruit set. Even after the June drop, there are too many apples left on the branches. Grow more than a few of these trees and you'll spend the summer hand-thinning. Have you seen Comfort yet?"

"I already said no." Spur plucked a low-hanging cherry, which held its green stem, indicating it wasn't quite ripe; despite this, he popped it into his mouth. "Sour cherries aren't too far from harvest, I'd say." He spat the pit at the gosdogs. "They're pulling the entire regiment back to Cloyce Forest, which is where I'll catch up with them."

"Civic refreshment—you'll be busy." Cape wound up and pitched a cull into the next row of trees. As the pack hurtled after it, he backed down the ladder. "Although I wouldn't mind some help. You're home for how long?"

"Just the week."

He hefted the ladder and pivoted it into the next tree. "Not much time."

"No."

He was about to climb up again when he realized that he had yet to greet his only son. "I'm glad you're safe, Prosper," he said, placing a hand on his shoulder. "But I still don't understand about the train." He held Spur at arm's length. "You got off why?"

Spur was desperate to change the subject. "DiDa, I know you don't want to hear this but Comfort and I are probably going to get divorced."

Cape grimaced and let go of Spur. "Probably?" He set his foot on the bottom rung.

"Yes." The gosdogs were back already, swarming around the ladder, downy feathers flying. "I'm sorry." Spur stepped away.

"Prosper, you know my feelings about this." He mounted the ladder. "But then everyone knows I'm a simple fool when it comes to keeping a woman."

Cape Leung had been saying things like that ever since Spur's mother left him. On some days he bemoaned the failure of his marriage as a wound that had crippled him for life, on others he preened as if surviving it were his one true distinction. As a young man, Spur had thought these were merely poses and had resented his father for keeping his feelings about Spur's mother in a tangle. Now, Spur thought maybe he understood.

"Comfort was never comfortable here," Spur said morosely. "I blame myself for that. But I don't think she was born to be a farmer's wife. Never was, never will be."

"Are you sure?" Cape sucked air between his teeth as he leaned into the tree. "She's had a terrible shock, Prosper. Now this?"

"It isn't going to come as a shock," he said, his voice tight. His father had far too many reasons for wanting Spur to make his marriage work. He had always liked both of the Joerly kids and had loved the way Comfort had remade both Diligence Cottage and his only son. Cape was impatient for grandchildren. And then there was the matter of the land, once agreeably complicated, now horribly simple. Ever since they had been kids, it had been a running joke around the village that someday Spur would marry Comfort and unite the Joerly farmstead with the Leung holdings, immediately adjacent to the east. Of course, everyone knew it wouldn't happen quite that way, because of Vic. But now Vic was dead.

"When will you see her?"

"I don't know," said Spur. "Soon. Anyway, it's been a long day for me. I'm going in."

"Come back to the house for supper?" said Cape.

"No, I'm too tired. I'll scrape up something to eat in the cottage."

"You won't have to look too hard." He grinned. "Your fans stopped by this morning to open the place up. I'm sure they left some goodies. I've been telling the neighbors that you were due home today." He dropped another cull to the gosdogs. "Now that I think about it, I should probably ride into town to tell folks not to meet your train. I still can't believe you got a ride all the way from ... where did you say it was again?"

"What fans?"

"I think it must have been Gandy Joy who organized it; at least she was the one who came to the house to ask my permission." He stepped off the ladder into the tree to reach the highest branches. "But I saw the Velez girls waiting in the van, Peace Toba, Summer Millisap." He stretched for a particularly dense cluster of apples. "Oh, and after they left, I think Comfort might have stopped by the cottage."

✡ TEN

The refrigerator was stocked with a chicken and parsnip casserole, a pot of barley soup, half a dozen eggs, a little tub of butter, a slab of goat cheese and three bottles of root beer. There was a loaf of fresh onion rye bread and glass jars of homemade apricot and pear preserves on the counter. But what Spur ate for supper was pie. Someone had baked him two pies, a peach and an apple. He ate half of each, and washed them down with root beer. Why not? There was nobody around to scold him and he was too tired to heat up the soup or the casserole, much less to eat it. Eating pie took no effort at all. Besides, he hadn't had a decent slice of pie since he had left Littleton. The niceties of baking were beyond the field kitchens of the Corps of Firefighters.

Afterward he poured himself a tumbler of applejack and sat at the kitchen table, trying to decide who had brought what. The barley soup felt like an offering from sturdy Peace

Toba. Gandy Joy knew he had a developed a secret weakness for root beer, despite growing up in a farmstead that lived and died by cider. The Millisaps had the largest herd of goats in town. He wasn't sure who had made the casserole, although he would have bet it wasn't the Velez sisters. Casseroles were too matronly for the Velezes. They were in their early twenties and single and a little wild — at least by Littleton's standards. They had to be, since they were searching for romance in a village of just over six hundred souls. Everyone said that they would probably move to Longwalk someday, or even to Heart's Wall, which would break their parents' hearts. He was guessing that the pies had come from their kitchen. A well-made pie was as good as a love letter. But would the Velez sisters just assume he and Comfort were finally going to split? Comfort must have decided on her own and was telling people in the village. Then Spur remembered that Sly had said he had heard something. And if Sly knew, then everyone knew. In a nosy village like Littleton, if a kid skinned his knee playing baseball, at least three moms fell out of trees waving bandages.

Spur put the food away and washed the dishes, after which there was no reason to stay in the kitchen. But he lingered for a while, trying to avoid the memories which whispered to him from the other rooms of the cottage. He remembered his stern grandparents ghosting around the wood stove in their last years. He remembered boarding Diligence Cottage up after GiGo died, the lumpy furniture and the threadbare carpet receding into the gloom. And then he and Comfort pulling the boards down and rediscovering their new home. The newlyweds had moved almost all of GiGo and GiGa's things to the barn, where they moldered to this day. Spur and Comfort had dusted and cleaned and scraped and painted everything in the empty cottage. He remembered sitting on the floor with his back to the wall of the parlor, looking at the one lonely chair they owned. Comfort had cuddled beside him, because she said that if there wasn't room for both of them on the chair then neither would sit. He had kissed her then. There had been a lot of kissing in those days. In fact, Comfort had made love to him in every room of the cottage. It was her way of declaring ownership and of exorcising the disapproving spirits of the old folks.

Now that she was about to pass out of his life, Spur thought that Comfort might have been too ferocious a lover for his tastes. Sometimes it was all he could do to stay with her in bed. Occasionally her passion alarmed him, although he would never have admitted this to himself while they were together. It would have been unmanly. But just before he had volunteered for the Corps, when things had already begun to go wrong, he had felt as if there was always another man standing next them, watching. Not anyone real, but rather Comfort's idea of a lover. Spur knew by then he wasn't that man. He had just been a placeholder for whoever it was she was waiting for.

Finally he left the kitchen. The women who had opened Diligence Cottage had done their best, but there was no air to work with on this close July night. The rooms were stale and hot. He sat out on the porch until the needlebugs drove him inside. Then he propped a fan in either window of the bedroom and dumped his kit out onto the bedspread. What did he have to wear that was cool? He picked up a T-shirt but then smelled the tang of smoke still clinging to it. He dropped it onto the bed and chuckled mirthlessly. He was home; he could put on his own clothes. He opened the dresser drawer and pulled out the shorts that Comfort had bought for his birthday and a gauzy blue shirt. The pants were loose and slid down his hips. He had lost weight in the firefight and even more in the hospital. Too much heartbreak. Not enough pie.

Then, against his better judgment, he crossed the bedroom to Comfort's dresser and began to open drawers. He had never understood why she abandoned everything she owned when she left him. Did it mean that she was planning to come back? Or that she was completely rejecting their life together? He didn't touch anything, just looked at her panties, black and navy blue and gray — no pastels or patterns for his girl. Then the balled socks, sleeveless blouses, shirts with the arms folded behind them, heavy workpants, lightweight sweaters. And in the bottom drawer the jade pajamas of black-market material so sheer that it would slip from her body if he even thought about tugging at it.

"Not exactly something a farmer's wife would wear." Spur spoke aloud just to hear a voice; the dense silence of the cottage was making him edgy. "At least, not this farmer's wife."

Now that he was losing Comfort, Spur realized that the

only person in his family was his father. It struck him that he had no memories of his father in the cottage. He could see Cape in the dining room of the big house or the library or dozing in front of the tell. Alone, always alone.

Spur had a bad moment then. He stepped into the bathroom, and splashed some cold water on his face. He would have to remarry or he would end up like his father. He tried to imagine kissing Bell Velez, slipping a hand under her blouse, but he couldn't.

"Knock, knock." A woman called from the parlor. "Your father claims you're back." It was Gandy Joy.

"Just a minute." Spur swiped at his dripping face with the hand towel. As he strode from the bedroom, the smile on his face was genuine. He was grateful to Gandy Joy for rescuing him from the silence and his dark mood.

She was a small, round woman with flyaway hair that was eight different shades of gray. She had big teeth and an easy smile. Her green sundress exposed the wrinkled skin of her wide shoulders and arms; despite farm work she was still as fair as the flesh of an apple. Spur had been mothered by many of the women of Littleton as a boy, but Gandy Joy was the one who meant the most to him. He had to stoop over slightly to hug her.

"Prosper." She squeezed him so hard it took his breath away. "My lovely boy, you're safe."

"Thank you for opening the cottage," he said. "But how did you find everything?" She smelled like lilacs and he realized that she must have perfumed herself just for him.

"Small house." She stepped back to take him in. "Not many places a thing can be."

Spur studied her as well; she seemed to have aged five years in the ten months since he'd seen her last. "Big enough, especially for one."

"I'm sorry, Prosper."

When Spur saw the sadness shadow her face, he knew that she had heard something. She was, after all, the village virtuator. He supposed he should have been relieved that Comfort was letting everyone know she wanted a divorce, since that was what he wanted too. Instead he just felt hollow. "What has she told you?"

Gandy Joy just shook her head. "You two have to talk."

He thought about pressing her, but decided to let it drop. "Have a seat, Gandy. Can I get you anything? There's applejack." He steered her toward the sofa. "And root beer."

"No thanks." She nodded at her wooden-bead purse, which he now noticed against the bolster of the sofa. "I brought communion."

"Really?" he said, feigning disappointment. "Then you're only here on business?"

"I'm here for more reasons than you'll ever know." She gave him a playful tap on the arm. "And keeping souls in communion is my calling, lovely boy, not my business." She settled on the sofa next to her purse and he sat facing her on the oak chair that had once been his only stick of furniture.

"How long are you with us?" She pulled out three incense burners and set them on the cherry wood table that Comfort had ordered all the way from Providence.

"A week." Spur had seen Gandy Joy's collection of incense burners, but he had never known her to use three at once for just two people. "I'll catch up with the squad in Cloyce Forest. Easy work for a change; just watching the trees grow." He considered three excessive; after all, he had accepted communion regularly with the other firefighters.

"We weren't expecting you so soon." She slipped the aluminum case marked with the seal of the Transcendent State from her purse. "You didn't come on the train."

"No."

She selected a communion square from the case. She touched it to her forehead, the tip of her nose and her lips and then placed it on edge in the incense burner. She glanced up at him and still the silence stretched. "Just no?" she said finally. "That's all?"

Spur handed her the crock of matches kept especially for communion. "My father told you to ask, didn't he?"

"I'm old, Prosper." Her smile was crooked. "I've earned the right to be curious." She repeated the ritual with the second communion square.

"You have. But he really wants to know."

"He always does." She set the third communion in its burner. "But then everybody understands about that particular bend in Capability's soul." She selected a match from the crock and struck it.

Now it was Spur's turn to wait. "So aren't you going to ask me about the train?"

"I was, but since you have something to hide, I won't." She touched the fire to each of the three squares and they caught immediately, the oils in the communion burning with an eager yellow flame. "I don't really care, Spur. I'm just happy that you're back and safe." She blew the flames out on each of the squares, leaving a glowing edge. "Make the most of your time with us."

Spur watched the communion smoke uncoil in the still air of his parlor. Then, as much to please Gandy Joy as to re-establish his connection with his village, he leaned forward and breathed deeply. The fumes that filled his nose were harsh at first, but wispier and so much sweeter than the strangling smoke of a burn. As he settled back into his chair, he got the subtle accents: the yeasty aroma of bread baking, a whiff of freshly split oak and just a hint of the sunshine scent of a shirt fresh off the clothesline. He could feel the communion smoke fill his head and touch his soul. It bound him as always to the precious land and the cottage where his family had made a new life, the orderly Leung farmstead, his home town and of course to this woman who loved him more than his mother ever had and his flinty father who couldn't help the way he was and faithful Sly Sawatdee and generous Leaf Benkleman and droll Will Sambusa and steadfast Peace Toba and the entire Velez family who had always been so generous to him and yes, even his dear Comfort Rose Joerly, who was leaving him but who was nonetheless a virtuous citizen of Littleton.

He shivered when he noticed Gandy Joy watching him. No

doubt she was trying to gauge whether he had fully accepted communion. "Thank you," he said, "for all the food."

She nodded, satisfied. "You're welcome. We just wanted to show how proud we are of you. This is your village, after all, and you're our Prosper and we want you to stay with us always."

He chuckled nervously. Why did everyone think he was going somewhere?

She leaned forward, and lowered her voice. "But I have to say there was more than a little competition going on over the cooking." She chuckled. "Bets were placed on which dish you'd eat first."

"Bets?" Spur found the idea of half a dozen women competing to please him quite agreeable. "And what did you choose?"

"After I saw everything laid out, I was thinking that you'd start in on pie. After all, there wasn't going to be anyone to tell you no."

Spur laughed. "Pie was all I ate. But don't tell anyone."

She tapped her forefinger to her lips and grinned.

"So I'm guessing that the Velez girls made the pies?"

"There was just the one — an apple, I think is what Bell said."

"I found two on the counter: apple and a peach."

"Really?" Gandy sat back on the couch. "Someone else must have dropped it off after we left."

"Might have been Comfort," said Spur. "DiDa said he thought she stopped by. I was expecting to find a note."

"Comfort was here?"

"She lives here," said Spur testily. "At least, all her stuff is here."

Gandy took a deep breath over the incense burners and held it in for several moments. "I'm worried about her," she said finally. "She hasn't accepted communion since we heard about Vic. She keeps to herself and when we go to visit her at home, she's as friendly as a brick. There's mourning and then there's self-pity, Prosper. She's been talking about selling the farmstead, moving away. We've lost poor Victor, we don't want to lose her too. Littleton wouldn't be the same without the Joerlys. When you see her, whatever you two decide, make sure she knows that."

Spur almost groaned then, but the communion had him in its benevolent grip. If citizens didn't help one another, there would be no Transcendent State. "I'll do my best," he said, his voice tight.

"Oh, I know you will, my lovely boy. I know it in my soul."

✧ ELEVEN

Things do not change; we change.
— JOURNAL, 1850

The High Gregory sat next to Spur in the bed of the Sawat-dees' truck, their backs against the cab, watching the dust billow behind them. Sly and Ngonda rode up front. As the truck jolted down Blue Valley Road, Spur could not help but see the excitement on the High Gregory's face. The dirt track was certainly rough, but the boy was bouncing so high Spur was worried that he'd fly over the side. He was even making Sly nervous, and the old farmer was usually as calm as moss. But then Sly Sawatdee didn't make a habit of giving rides to upsiders. He kept glancing over his shoulder at the High Gregory through the open rear slider.

Spur had no doubt that his cover story for the High Gregory and Ngonda was about to unravel. The High Gregory had decided to wear purple overalls with about twenty brass buttons. Although there was nothing wrong with his black T-shirt, the bandana knotted around his neck was a pink disaster embellished with cartoons of beets and carrots and corn on the cob. At least he had used some upsider trick to disguise the color of his eyes. Ngonda's clothes weren't quite as odd, but they too were a problem. Spur had seen citizens wearing flair jackets and high-collar shirts — but not on a hot summer Sunday and not in Littleton. Ngonda was dressed for a meeting at the Cooperative's Office of Diplomacy in Concord. Spur's only hope was to whisk them both to Diligence Cottage and either hide them there or find them something more appropriate to wear.

"Tell me about the gosdogs," said the High Gregory.

Spur leaned closer, trying to hear him over the roar of the truck's engine, the clatter of its suspension and the crunch of tires against the dirt road. "Say again?"

"The gosdogs," shouted the High Gregory. "One of your native species. You know, four-footed, feathered, they run in packs."

"Gosdogs, yes. What do you want to know?"

"You eat them."

"I don't." The High Gregory seemed to be waiting for him to elaborate, but Spur wasn't sure what he wanted to know exactly. "Other citizens do, but the browns only. The other breeds are supposed to be too stringy."

"And when you kill them, do they know they're about to die? How do you do it?"

"I don't." Spur had never slaughtered a gosdog; Cape didn't believe in eating them. However, Spur had slaughtered chickens and goats and helped once with a bull. Butchering was one of the unpleasant chores that needed doing on a farm, like digging postholes or mucking out the barn.

"They don't suffer."

"Really? That's good to know." The High Gregory did not look convinced. "How smart do you think they are?"

At that moment Sly stepped on the brakes and swung the steering wheel; the truck bumped onto the smooth pavement of Civic Route 22.

"Not very," said Spur. With the road noise abating, his voice carried into the cab.

"Not very what?" said Constant Ngonda.

The High Gregory propped himself up to speak through the open window. "I was asking Spur how smart the gosdogs are. I couldn't find much about them, considering. Why is that, do you suppose?"

"The ComExplore Survey Team rated them just 6.4 on the Peekay Animal Intelligence Scale," said Ngonda. "A goat has more brains."

"Yes, I found that," said the High Gregory, "but what's interesting is that the first evaluation was the only one ever done. And it would have been very much in the company's interests to test them low, right? And of course it made no sense for your pukpuks to bother with a follow-up test. And now your Transcendent State has a stake in keeping that rating as it is."

"Are you suggesting some kind of conspiracy?" Ngonda was working his way to a fine outrage. "That we're deliberately abusing an intelligent species?"

"I'm just asking questions, friend Constant. And no, I'm not saying they're as smart as humans, no, no, never. But suppose they were retested and their intelligence was found to be ... let's say 8.3. Or even 8.1. The Thousand Worlds might want to see them protected."

"Protected?" The deputy's voice snapped through the window.

"Why, don't you think that would be a good idea? You'd just have to round them up and move them to a park or something. Let them loose in their native habitat."

"There is no native habitat left on Walden." Spur noticed that Sly was so intent on the conversation that he was coasting down the highway. "Except maybe underwater." A westbound oil truck was catching up to them fast.

"We could build one then," said the High Gregory cheerfully. "The L'ung could raise the money. They need something to do."

"Can I ask you something?" Ngonda had passed outrage and was well on his way to fury.

"Yes, friend Constant. Of course."

"How old are you?"

"Twelve standard. My birthday is next month. I don't want a big party this year. It's too much work."

"They know themselves in the mirror," said Sly.

"What?" Ngonda was distracted from whatever point he was about to make. "What did you just say?"

"When one of them looks at his reflection, he recognizes himself." Sly leaned back toward the window as he spoke. "We had this brood, a mother and three pups, who stayed indoors with us last winter. They were house-trained, mostly." The truck slowed to a crawl. "So my granddaughter Brookie is playing dress-up with the pups one night and the silly little pumpkin decides to paint one all over with grape juice. Said she was trying to make the first purple gosdog — her father babies her, don't you know? But she actually stains the right rear leg before her mother catches her out. And when Brookie lets the poor thing loose, it galumphs to the mirror and backs up to see its grapy leg. Then it gets to whimpering and clucking and turning circles like they do when they're upset." Sly checked the rearview mirror and noticed the oil truck closing in on them for the first time. "I was there, saw it clear as tap water. The idea that it knew who it was tipped me over for a couple of days." He put two wheels onto the shoulder of CR22 and waved the truck past. "It's been a hardship, but I've never eaten a scrap of gosdog since."

"That's the most ridiculous thing I've ever heard," said Ngonda.

"Lots of citizens feel that way," said Spur.

"As is their right. But to jump to conclusions based on this man's observations...."

"I don't want to jump, friend Constant," said the High Gregory. "Let's not jump."

Although the deputy was ready to press his argument, nobody else spoke and gradually he subsided. Sly pulled back onto CR22 and drove the rest of the way at a normal pace. They passed the rest of the trip in silence; the wind seemed to whip Spur's thoughts right out of his head.

✦

As they turned off Jane Powder Street onto the driveway of the cottage, Sly called back to him. "Looks like you've got company."

Spur rubbed the back of his neck in frustration. Who told the townsfolk that he wanted them to come visiting? He leaned over the side of the truck but couldn't see anyone until they parked next to the porch. Then he spotted the scooter leaning against the barn.

If it was really in the High Gregory's power to make luck, then what he was brewing up for Spur so far was pure misfortune. It was Comfort's scooter.

The High Gregory stood up in the back of the truck and turned around once, surveying the farmstead. "This is your home, Spur." He said it not as a question but as a statement, as if Spur were the one seeing it for the first time. "I understand now why you would want to live so far from everything. It's like a poem here."

Constant Ngonda opened the door and stepped down onto the dusty drive. From his expression, the deputy appeared to have formed a different opinion of the cottage. However, he was enough of a diplomat to keep it to himself. He clutched a holdall to his chest and was mounting the stairs to the porch when he noticed that no one else had moved from the truck.

They were watching Comfort stalk toward them from the barn, so clearly in a temper that heat seemed to shimmer off her in the morning swelter.

"That woman looks angry as lightning," said Sly. "You want me to try to get in her way?"

"No," said Spur. "She'd probably just knock you over."

"But this is your Comfort?" said the High Gregory. "The wife that you don't live with anymore. This is so exciting, just what I was hoping for. She's come for a visit — maybe to welcome you back?"

"I'm not expecting much of a welcome," said Spur. "If you'll excuse me, I should talk to her. Sly, if you wouldn't mind staying a few minutes, maybe you could take Constant and young Lucky here inside. There's plenty to eat."

"Lucky," said the High Gregory, repeating the name they had agreed on for him, as if reminding himself to get into character. "Hello, friend Comfort," he called. "I'm Lucky. Lucky Ngonda."

She shook the greeting off and kept bearing down on them. His wife was a slight woman, with fine features and eyes dark tas currants. Her hair was long and sleek and black. She was wearing a sleeveless, yellow gingham dress that Spur had never seen before. Part of her new wardrobe, he thought, her new life. When he had been in love with her, Spur had thought that Comfort was pretty. But now, seeing her for the first time in months, he decided that she was merely delicate. She did not look strong enough for the rigors of life on a farm.

Spur opened the tailgate and the High Gregory jumped from the back of the truck. Ngonda came back down the stairs to be introduced to Comfort. Spur was handing the High Gregory's bag down to Sly as she drew herself up in front of them.

"Gandy Joy said you wanted to see me first thing in the morning." She did not waste time on introductions. "I didn't realize that I'd be interrupting a party."

"Comfort," said Spur, "I'm sorry." He stopped himself then, chagrined at how easily he fell into the old pattern. When they were together, he was always apologizing.

"Morning, sweet corn," said Sly. "Not that much of a party, I'm afraid."

"But there are snacks inside," the High Gregory said. "This is such a beautiful place you two have. I've just met Spur myself, but I'm pretty sure he's going to be happy here someday. My name is Lucky Ngonda." He held out his hand to her. "We're supposed to shake but first you have to say your name."

Comfort had been so fixated on Spur that she had brushed by the High Gregory. Now she scrutinized him in all his purple glory and her eyes went wide. "Why are you dressed like that?"

"Is something wrong?" He glanced down at his overalls. "I'm dressed to visit my friend Spur." He patted his bare head. "It's the hat, isn't it? I'm supposed to be wearing a hat."

"Constant Ngonda, a friend of Spur's from the Ninth." Ngonda oozed between them. "I apologize for intruding; I know you have some important things to discuss. Why don't we give you a chance to catch up now. My nephew and I will be glad to wait inside." He put an arm around the High Gregory's shoulder and aimed him at the porch.

"Wait," said the High Gregory. "I thought I was your cousin."

"Take as long as you want, Spur," Ngonda said as he hustled the boy off. "We'll be fine."

Sly shook his head in disbelief. "I'll make sure they don't get into trouble." He started after them.

"There are pies in the refrigerator," Spur called after him. "Most of an apple pie and just a couple slices of a peach." He steeled himself and turned back to Comfort. "My father said you were here the other day." He aimed a smile at her but it bounced off. "You made my favorite pie."

"Who are those people?" Her eyes glittered with suspicion. "The boy is strange. Why have you brought them here?"

"Let's walk." He took her arm and was surprised when she went along without protest. He felt the heat of her glare cooling as they strode away from the cottage. "I did have a chat with Gandy Joy," he said. "She said you were feeling pretty low."

"I have the right to feel however I feel," she said stiffly.

"You haven't been accepting communion."

"Communion is what they give you so you feel smart about acting stupid. Tell her that I don't need some busybody blowing smoke in my eyes to keep me from seeing what's wrong." She stopped and pulled him around to face her. "We're getting divorced, Spur."

"Yes," He held her gaze. "I know." He wanted to hug her

or maybe shake her. Touch her long, black hair. Instead his hands hung uselessly by his sides. "But I'm still concerned about you."

"Why?"

"You've been talking about moving away."

She turned and started walking again. "I can't run a farm by myself."

"We could help you, DiDa and I." He caught up with her. "Hire some of the local kids. Maybe bring in a tenant from another village."

"And how long do you think that would work for? If you want to run my farm, Spur, buy it from me."

"Your family is an important part of this place. The whole village wants you to stay. Everyone would pitch in."

She chuckled grimly. "Everyone wanted us to get married. They want us to stay together. I'm tired of having everyone in my life."

He wasn't going to admit to her that he felt the same way sometimes. "Where will you go?"

"Away."

"Just away?"

"I miss him, I really do. But I don't want to live anywhere near Vic's grave."

Spur kicked a stone across the driveway and said nothing for several moments. "You're sure it's not me you want to get away from?"

"No, Spur. That's one thing I am sure of."

"When did you decide all this?"

"Spur, I'm not mad at you." Impulsively, she went up on tiptoes and aimed a kiss at the side of his face. She got mostly air, but their cheeks brushed, her skin hot against his. "I like you, especially when you're like this, so calm and thoughtful. You're the best of this lot and you've always been sweet to me. It's just that I can't live like this anymore."

"I like you too, Comfort. Last night, after I accepted communion—"

"Enough. We like each other. We should stop there, it's a good place to be." She bumped up against him. "Now tell me about that boy. He isn't an upsider, is he?"

She shot him a challenging look and he tried to bear up under the pressure of her regard. They walked in silence while he decided what he could say about Ngonda and the High Gregory. "Can you keep a secret?"

She sighed. "You know you're going to tell me, so get to it."

They had completely circled the cottage. Spur spotted the High Gregory watching them from a window. He turned Comfort toward the barn. "Two days ago, when I was still in the hospital, I started sending greetings to the upside." He waved off her objections. "Don't ask, I don't know why exactly, other than that I was bored. Anyway, the boy answered one of them. He's the High Gregory of the L'ung, Phosphorescence of something or other, I forget what. He's from Kenning in the Theta Persei system and I'm guessing he's pretty important, because the next thing I knew, he qiced himself to Walden and had me pulled off a train."

He told her about the hover and Memsen and the kids of the L'ung and how he was being forced to show the High Gregory his village. "Oh, and he supposedly makes luck."

"What does that mean?" said Comfort. "How does somebody make luck?"

"I don't know exactly. But Memsen and the L'ung are all convinced that he does it, whatever it is."

They had wandered into GiGa's flower garden. Comfort had tried to make it her own after they had moved in. However, she'd had neither the time nor the patience to tend persnickety plants and so grew only daylilies and hostas and rugose roses. After a season of neglect, even these tough flowers were losing ground to the bindweed and quackgrass and spurge.

Spur sat on the fieldstone bench that his grandfather had built for his grandmother. He tapped on the seat for her to join him. She hesitated then settled at the far end, twisting to face him.

"He acts too stupid to be anyone important," she said. "What about that slip he made about being the cousin and not the nephew. Are the people on his world idiots?"

"Maybe he intended to say it." Spur leaned forward and pulled a flat clump of spurge from the garden. "After all, he's wearing those purple overalls; he's really not trying very hard to pretend he's a citizen." He knocked the dirt off the roots and left it to shrivel in the sun. "What if he wanted me to tell you who he was and decided to make it happen? I think he's used to getting his own way."

"So what does he want with us?" Her expression was unreadable.

"I'm not sure. I think what Memsen was telling me is that he has come here to see how his being here changes us." He shook his head. "Does that make any sense?"

"It doesn't have to," she said. "He's from the upside. They don't think the same way we do."

"Maybe so." It was a commonplace that had been drilled into them in every self-reliance class they had ever sat through. It was, after all, the reason that Chairman Winter had founded Walden. But now that he had actually met upsiders — Memsen and the High Gregory and the L'ung — he wasn't sure that their ways were so strange. But this wasn't the time to argue the point. "Look, Comfort, I have my own reason for telling you all this," he said. "I need help with him. At first I thought he was just going to pretend to be one of us and take a quiet look at the village. Now I'm thinking he wants to be discovered so he can make things happen. So I'm going to try to keep him busy here if I can. It's just for one day; he said he'd leave in the morning."

"And you believe that?"

"I'd like to." He dug at the base of a dandelion with his fingers and pried it out of the ground with the long taproot intact. "What other choice do I have?" He glanced back at the cottage but couldn't see the High Gregory in the window anymore. "We'd better get back."

She put a hand on his arm. "First we have to talk about Vic."

Spur paused, considering. "We can do that if you want." He studied the dandelion root as if it held the answers to all his problems. "We probably should. But it's hard, Comfort. When I was in the hospital the upsiders did something to me. A kind of treatment that...."

She squeezed his arm and then let go. "There's just one thing I have to know. You were with him at the end. At least, that's what we heard. You reported his death."

"It was quick," said Spur. "He didn't suffer." This was a lie he had been preparing to tell her ever since he had woken up in the hospital.

"That's good. I'm glad." She swallowed. "Thank you. But did he say anything? At the end, I mean."

"Say? Say what?"

"You have to understand that after I moved back home, I found that Vic had changed. I was shocked when he volunteered for the Corps because he was actually thinking of leaving Littleton. Maybe Walden too. He talked a lot about going to the upside." She clutched her arms to her chest so tightly that she seemed to shrink. "He didn't believe — you can't tell anyone about this. Promise?"

Spur shut his eyes and nodded. He knew what she was going to say. How could he not? Nevertheless, he dreaded hearing it.

Her voice shrank as well. "He had sympathy for the puk-puks. Not for the burning, but he used to say that we didn't need to cover every last scrap of Walden with forest. He talked about respecting..."

Without warning, the nightmare leapt from some darkness in his soul like some ravening predator. It chased him through a stand of pine; trees exploded like firecrackers. Sparks bit through his civvies and stung him. He could smell burning hair. His hair.

But he didn't want to smell his hair burning. Spur was trying desperately to get back to the bench in the garden, back to Comfort, but she kept pushing him deeper into the nightmare.

"After we heard he'd been killed, I went to his room..."

He beckoned and for a moment Spur thought it might not be Vic after all as the anguished face shimmered in the heat of the burn. Vic wouldn't betray them, would he?

"It was his handwriting. . . ."

Spur had to dance to keep his shoes from catching fire, and he had no escape, no choice, no time. The torch spread his arms wide and Spur stumbled into his embrace and with an angry whoosh they exploded together into flame. Spur felt his skin crackle. . . .

And he screamed.

✧ Twelve

We are paid for our suspicions by finding what we suspected.
– A WEEK ON THE CONCORD AND MERRIMACK RIVERS

Everyone said that he had nothing to be embarrassed about, but Spur was nonetheless deeply ashamed. He had been revealed as unmanly. Weak and out of control. He had no memory of how he had come to be laid out on the couch in his own parlor. He couldn't remember if he had wept or cursed or just fainted and been dragged like a sack of onions across the yard into the cottage. When he emerged from the nightmare, all he knew was that his throat was raw and his cheeks were hot. The others were all gathered around him, trying not to look worried but not doing a very convincing job of it. He wasn't sure which he minded more: that the strangers had witnessed his breakdown, or that his friends and neighbors had.

When he sat up, a general alarm rippled among the onlookers. When he tried to stand, Sly pressed him back onto the couch with a firm grip on the shoulder. Comfort fetched him a glass of water. She was so distraught that her hand shook as she offered it to him. He took a sip, more to satisfy the others than to quench his own thirst. They needed to think they were helping, even though the best thing they could have done for him then — go away and leave him alone — was the one thing they were certain not to do.

"Maybe I should call Dr. Niss." Spur's laugh was as light as ashes. "Ask for my money back."

"You're right." Constant Ngonda lit up at the thought, then realized that his enthusiasm was unseemly. "I mean, shouldn't we notify the hospital?" he said, eyeing the tell on the parlor wall. "They may have concerns."

Spur knew that the deputy would love to have him whisked away from Littleton, in the hopes that the High Gregory and the L'ung would follow. He wondered briefly if that might not be for the best, but then he had been humiliated enough that morning. "There's nothing to worry about."

"Good," said Ngonda. "I'm happy to hear that, Spur. Do you mind, I promised to check in with the Cooperative when we arrived?" Without waiting for a reply, Ngonda bustled across the parlor to the kitchen. Meanwhile, the High Gregory had sprawled onto a chair, his legs dangling over the armrest. He was flipping impatiently through a back issue of Didactic Arts' *True History Comix* without really looking at the pages. Spur thought he looked even more squirmy than usual, as if he knew there was someplace else he was supposed to be. Sly Sawatdee had parked himself next to Spur. His hands were folded in his lap, his eyelids were heavy and he hummed to himself from time to time, probably thinking about fishing holes and berry patches and molasses cookies.

"I am so sorry, Spur," said Comfort. "I just didn't realize." It was the third time she had apologized. She wasn't used to apologizing and she didn't do it very well. Meanwhile her anguish was smothering him. Her face was pale, her mouth was as crooked as a scar. What had he said to her? He couldn't remember but it must have been awful. There was a quiet desperation in her eyes that he had never seen before. It scared him.

Spur set the glass of water on the end table. "Listen, Comfort, there is nothing for you to be sorry about." He was the one who had fallen apart, after all. "Let's just forget it, all right? I'm fine now." To prove it, he stood up.

Sly twitched but did not move to pull him back onto the couch again. "Have enough air up there, my hasty little sparrow?"

"I'm fine," he repeated and it was true. Time to put this by and move on. Change the subject. "Who wants to see the orchard? Lucky?"

"If you don't mind," said Sly. "My bones are in no mood for a hike. But I'll make us lunch."

"I'll come," said Ngonda.

Comfort looked as if she wanted to beg off, but guilt got the better of her.

They tramped around the grounds, talking mostly of farm matters. After they had admired the revived orchard, inspected the weed-choked garden, toured the barn, played with the pack of gosdogs that had wandered over from the big house and began to follow them everywhere, walked the boundaries of the corn field which Cape had planted in clover until Spur was ready to farm again, they hiked through the woods down to Mercy's Creek.

"We take some irrigation water from the creek, but the Joerlys own the rights, so there's water in our end of the creek pretty much all year long." Spur pointed. "There's a pool in the woods where Comfort and I used to swim when we were kids. It might be a good place to cool off this afternoon."

"And so you and Spur were neighbors?" The High Gregory had been trying to draw Comfort out all morning, without much success. "You grew up together like me and my friends. I was hoping to bring them along but Uncle Constant Ngonda said there were too many of them. Your family is still living on the farm?"

"Mom died. She left everything to us. Now Vic's dead."

"Yes, Spur said that your brother was a brave firefighter. I know that you are very sad about it, but I see much more luck ahead for you."

She leaned against a tree and stared up at the sky.

"There used to be a pukpuk town in these woods." Spur was itching to move on. "They built all along the creek. It's overgrown now, but we could go look at the ruins."

The High Gregory stepped off the bank onto a flat stone that stuck out of the creek. "And your father?"

"He left," Comfort said dully.

"When they were little," Spur said quickly. He knew that Comfort did not like even to think about her father, much less talk about him with strangers. Park Nen had married into the Joerly family. Not only was his marriage to Rosie Joerly stormy, but he was also a loner who had never quite adjusted to village ways. "The last we heard Park was living in Freeport."

The High Gregory picked his way across the creek on steppingstones. "He was a pukpuk, no?" His foot slipped and he windmilled his arms to keep his balance.

"Who told you that?" If Comfort had been absent-minded before, she was very much present now.

"I forget." He crossed back over the stream in four quick hops. "Was it you, Uncle?"

Ngonda licked his lips nervously. "I've never heard of this person."

"Then maybe it was Spur."

Spur would have denied it if Comfort had given him the chance.

"He never knew." Her voice was sharp. "Nobody did." She confronted the boy. "Don't play games with me, upsider." He tried to back away but she pursued him. "Why do you care about my father? Why are you here?"

"Are you crazy?" Ngonda caught the High Gregory as he stumbled over a rock and then thrust the boy behind him. "This is my nephew Lucky."

"She knows, friend Constant." The High Gregory peeked out from behind the deputy's flair jacket. He was glowing with excitement. "Spur told her everything."

"Oh, no." Ngonda slumped. "This isn't going well at all."

"Memsen gave us all research topics for the trip here to

meet Spur," said the High Gregory. "Kai Thousandfold was assigned to find out about you. You'd like him; he's from Bellweather. He says that he's very worried about you, friend Comfort."

"Tell him to mind his own business."

Spur was aghast. "Comfort, I'm sorry, I didn't know. . . ."

"Be quiet, Spur. These upsiders are playing you for the fool that you are." Her eyes were wet. "I hardly knew my father and what I did know, I didn't like. Mom would probably still be alive if she hadn't been left to manage the farm by herself all those years." Her chin quivered; Spur had never seen her so agitated. "She told us that Grandma Nen was a pukpuk, but that she emigrated from the barrens long before my father was born and that he was brought up a citizen like anyone else." Tears streaked her face. "So don't think you understand anything about me because you found out about a dead woman who I never met."

With that she turned and walked stiff-legged back toward Diligence Cottage. She seemed to have shrunk since the morning, and now looked so insubstantial to Spur that a summer breeze might carry her off like milkweed. He knew there was more — much more — they had to talk about, but first they would have to find a new way to speak to each other. As she disappeared into the woods, he felt a twinge of nostalgia for the lost simplicity of their youth, when life really had been as easy as Chairman Winter promised it could be.

"I'm hungry." The High Gregory seemed quite pleased with himself. "Is it lunchtime yet?"

After he had spun out lunch for as long as he could, Spur was at a loss as to how to keep the High Gregory out of trouble. They had exhausted the sights of the Leung farmstead, short of going over to visit with his father in the big house. Spur considered it, but decided to save it for a last resort. He had hoped to spend the afternoon touring the Joerly farmstead, but now that was out of the question. As the High Gregory fidgeted about the cottage, picking things up and putting them down again, asking about family pix, opening cabinets and pulling out drawers, Spur proposed that they take a spin around Littleton in Sly's truck. A rolling tour, he told himself. No stops.

The strategy worked for most of an hour. At first the High Gregory was content to sit next to Spur in the back of the truck as he pointed out Littleton's landmarks and described the history of the village. They drove up Lamana Ridge Road to Lookover Point, from which they had a view of most of Littleton Commons. The village had been a Third Wave settlement, populated by the winners of the lottery of 2432. In the first years of settlement, the twenty-five founding families had worked together to construct the buildings of the Commons: the self-reliance school, athenaeum, communion lodge, town hall and Littleton's first exchange, where goods and services could be bought or bartered. The First Twenty-five had lived communally in rough barracks until the buildings on the Commons were completed, and then gradually moved out to their farmsteads as land was cleared and crews of carpenters put up the cottages and barns and sheds for each of the families. The Leungs had arrived in the Second Twenty-five four years afterward. The railroad had come through three years after that and most of the businesses of the first exchange moved from the Commons out to Shed Town by the train station. Sly drove them down the ridge and they bumped along back roads, past farms and fields and pastures. They viewed the Toba and Parochet and Velez farmsteads from a safe distance and passed Sambusa's lumberyard at the confluence of Mercy's Creek and the Swift River. Then they pulled back onto CR22.

The only way back to Diligence Cottage was through the Commons. "Drive by the barracks," Spur called to Sly in the cab. "We can stretch our legs there," he said to the High Gregory. "I'll show you how the First Twenty-five lived." One of the original barracks had been preserved as a historical museum across the lawn from the communion lodge. It was left open to any who wanted to view its dusty exhibits. Spur thought it the best possible choice for a stop; except for Founders' Day, the Chairman's birthday and Thanksgiving, nobody ever went there.

The Commons appeared to be deserted as they passed the buildings of the first exchange. These had been renovated into housing for those citizens of Littleton who didn't farm, like the teachers at the self-reliance school and Dr. Christopoulos and some of the elders, like Gandy Joy. They saw Doll Groth coming out of the athenaeum. Recognizing the truck, she gave Sly a neighborly wave, but when she spotted Spur in the back, she smiled and began to clap, raising her hands over her head. This so pleased the High Gregory that he stood up and started clapping back at her. Spur had to brace him to keep him from pitching over the side of the truck.

But Doll was the only person they saw. Spur couldn't believe his good fortune as they pulled up to the barracks, dust from the gravel parking lot swirling around them. The wind had picked up, but provided no relief from the midsummer heat. Spur's shirt stuck to his back where he had been leaning against the cab of the truck. Although he wasn't sure whether the High Gregory could sweat or not, the boy's face was certainly flushed. Ngonda looked as if he were liquefying inside his flair jacket. The weather fit Spur's latest plan neatly. He was hoping that after they had spent a half-hour in the hot and airless barracks, he might be able to persuade the High Gregory to return to Diligence Cottage for a swim in the creek. After that it would practically be suppertime. And after that they could watch the tell. Or he might teach the High Gregory some of the local card games. Spur had always been lucky at Fool All.

It wasn't until the engine of the Sawatdees' truck coughed and rattled and finally cut out that Spur first heard the whoop of the crowd. Something was going on at the ball fields next to the self-reliance school, just down the hill a couple hundred meters. He tried to usher the High Gregory into the barracks but it was too late. Spur thought there must be a lot of people down there. They were making a racket that was hard to miss.

The High Gregory cocked his head in the direction of the school and smiled. "Lucky us," he said. "We're just in time for Memsen."

✿ Thirteen

I associate this day, when I can remember it, with games of
base-ball played over behind the hills in the russet fields toward
Sleepy Hollow.
  – JOURNAL, 1856

"What is this?" hissed Ngonda.

Sly pulled his floppy hat off and wiped his forehead with it.
"Looks like a baseball game, city pants," said Sly.

The L'ung were in the field; with a sick feeling Spur
counted twelve of them in purple overalls and black T-shirts.
They must have arrived in the two vans that were parked
next to the wooden bleachers. Beside the vans was an array
of trucks, scooters and bicycles from the village. There must
have been a hundred citizens sitting in the bleachers and
another twenty or thirty prowling the edges of the field,
cheering the home team on. Match Klizzie had opened the
refreshment shed and was barbequing sausages. Gandy Joy
had set up her communion tent: Spur could see billows of
sweet white smoke whenever one of the villagers pulled back
the flap.

With many of the younger baseball regulars off at the firefight, the Littleton Eagles might have been undermanned. But Spur could see that some old-timers had come out of retirement to pull on the scarlet hose. Warp Kovacho was just stepping up to home base and Spur spotted Cape sitting on the strikers' bench, second from the inbox.

Betty Chief Twosalt shined the ball against her overalls as she peered in at Warp. "Where to, old sir?" She was playing feeder for the L'ung.

Warp swung the flat bat at belt level to show her just where he wanted the feed to cross home base. "Right here, missy," he said. "Then you better duck." They were playing with just two field bases, left and right. The banners fixed to the top of each basepole snapped in the stiffening breeze.

Betty nodded and then delivered the feed underhanded. It was slow and very fat but Warp watched it go by. The Pendragon Chromlis Furcifer was catching for the L'ung. She barehanded it and flipped it back to Betty.

"What's he waiting for?" grumbled the High Gregory. "That was perfect." He ignored Spur's icy stare.

"Just a smight lower next time, missy," said Warp, once again indicating his preference with the bat. "You got the speed right, now hit the spot."

Young Melody Velez was perched at the end of the topmost bleacher and noticed Spur passing beneath her. "He's here!" she cried. "Spur's here!"

Play stopped and the bleachers emptied as the villagers crowded around him, clapping him on the back and shaking his hand. In five minutes he'd been kissed more than he'd been kissed altogether in the previous year.

"So is this another one of your upsider friends?" Gandy Joy held the High Gregory at arms length, taking him in. "Hello, boy. What's your name?"

"I'm the High Gregory of Kenning," he said. "But my Walden name is Lucky, so I'd rather have you call me that."

Citizens nearby laughed nervously.

"Lucky you are then."

Gandy Hope Nakuru touched the pink bandana knotted around his neck. "Isn't this a cute scarf?" The High Gregory beamed.

Spur was astonished by it all. "But who told you that they're from the upside?" he said. "How did they get here? And why are you playing baseball?"

"Memsen brought them," said Peace Toba. "She said that you'd be along once we got the game going."

"And she was right." Little Jewel Parochet tugged at his shirt. "Spur, she said you flew in a hover. What was it like?"

"Maybe next time you can bring a guest along with you?" Melody Velez said, smiling. She brushed with no great subtlety against him.

Spur glanced about the thinning crowd; citizens were climbing back into the bleachers. "But where is Memsen?"

Peace Toba pointed; Memsen had only come out onto the field as far as right base when Constant Ngonda had captured her. He was waving his arms so frantically that he looked like he might take off and fly around the field. Memsen tilted her head so that her ear was practically on her shoulder. Then she saw Spur. She clicked her rings at him, a sly smile on her face. He knew he ought to be angry with her, but instead he felt buoyant, as if he had just set his splash pack down and stepped out of his field jacket. Whatever happened now, it wasn't his fault. He had done his best for his village.

"So this was what you were keeping from me." His father was chuckling. "I knew it had to be something. They're fine, your friends. You didn't need to worry." He hugged Spur and whispered into his ear. "Fine, but very strange. They're not staying are they?" He pulled back. "Prosper, we need your bat in this game. These kids are tough." He pointed at Kai Thousandfold "That one has an arm like a fire hose."

"No thanks," said Spur. "But you should get back to the game." He raised his arms over his head and waved to the bleachers. "Thank you all, thanks," he called to his well-wishers. They quieted down to listen. "If you're expecting some kind of speech, then you've got the wrong farmer. I'll just say that I'm glad to be home and leave it at that. All right?" The crowd made a murmur of assent. "Then play ball." They cheered. "And go Eagles!" They cheered louder.

"Can I play?" said the High Gregory. "This looks like fun." He straightened the strap of his overalls. "I can play, can't I? We have all kinds of baseball on Kenning. But your rules are different, right? Tell them to me."

"Why bother?" Spur was beginning to wonder if the High Gregory was playing him for a fool. "Looks like you're making them up as you go."

Her Grace, Jacqueline Kristof, put an arm around his

shoulder. "The ball is soft, so no gloves," she said, as she led him onto the field. "No tag outs either, you actually have to hit the runner with the ball. That's called a sting. No fouls and no..."

As the spectators settled into their seats, Spur found his way to Ngonda and Memsen. She wasn't wearing the standard L'ung overalls, but rather a plain green sundress with a floral print. She had washed the phosphorescent paint off her arms and pulled her hair back into a ponytail. But if Memsen was trying to look inconspicuous, then she had failed utterly. She was still the tallest woman on the planet.

"Talk to her," said Ngonda. "We had an agreement...."

"Which you broke," said Memsen. "What we agreed was that the High Gregory would visit Littleton and you'd let him make whatever luck you are destined to have. You promised to give him the run of the village —"

" — under Spur's supervision, Allworthy," interrupted Ngonda.

Betty Chief Twosalt delivered a feed and Warp watched it go by again. This did not sit well with the L'ung. "Delay of game, old sir," someone called.

Memsen turned from Ngonda to Spur. "As we were explaining to the deputy, the L'ung and I see everything that the High Gregory sees. So we know that you've introduced him to just two of your neighbors. You promised that he could meet the citizens of this village but then you've kept him isolated until now. He needs to be with people, Spur. Barns don't have luck. People do."

"It was my decision," said Spur. "I'll take the responsibility."

"And this was ours." She waved toward the field. "So?"

Ngonda snorted in disgust. "I need to call Concord. The Office of Diplomacy will be filing a protest with the Forum of the Thousand Worlds." He took a step away from them, then turned and waggled a finger at Memsen. "This is a clear violation of our Covenant, Allworthy. The L'ung will be recalled to Kenning."

As they watched Ngonda stalk off, Warp struck a grounder straight back at the feeder. Betty stabbed at it but it tipped off her fingers and rolled away at an angle. Little Senator Dowm pounced on it but held the throw because Warp already had a hand on the right base stake.

"Maybe I should've introduced the High Gregory to a few more people." Spur wondered if standing too close to Memsen might be affecting his perceptions. The very planet seemed to tilt slightly, as it had that afternoon when he and Leaf Benkleman had drunk a whole liter of her mother's prize applejack. "But why are we playing baseball?"

Memsen showed him her teeth in that way she had that wasn't anything like a smile. "Tolerance isn't something that the citizens of the Transcendent State seem to value. You've been taught that your way of life is better not only than that of the pukpuks, but than that of most of the cultures of the Thousand Worlds. Or have we misread the textbooks?"

Spur shook his head grimly.

"So." She pinched the air. "Deputy Ngonda was right to

point out that landing a hover on your Commons might have intimidated some people. We had to find some unthreatening way to arrive, justify our presence and meet your neighbors. The research pointed to baseball as a likely ploy. Your Eagles were champions of Hamilton County just two years ago and second runner-up in the Northeast in 2498."

"A ploy."

"A ploy to take advantage of your traditions. Your village is proud of its accomplishments in baseball. You're used to playing against strangers. And of course, we had an invitation from Spur Leung, the hero of the hour."

Livy Jayawardena hit a high fly ball that sailed over the heads of the midfielders. Kai Thousandfold, playing deep field, raced back and made an over-the-shoulder catch. Meanwhile Warp had taken off for left base. In his prime, he might have made it, but his prime had been when Spur was a toddler. Kai turned, set and fired; his perfect throw stung Warp right between the shoulder blades. Double play, inning over.

"I invited you?" said Spur. "When was that again?"

"Why, in the hospital where we saved your life. You kept claiming that the L'ung would offer no competition for your Eagles. You told Dr. Niss that you couldn't imagine losing a baseball game to upsiders, much less a bunch of children. Really, Spur, that was too much. We had to accept your challenge once you said that. So when we arrived at the town hall, we told our story to everyone we met. Within an hour the bleachers were full."

Spur was impressed. "And you thought of all this since yesterday?"

"Actually, just in the last few hours." She paused then, seemingly distracted. She made a low, repetitive pa-pa-pa-ptt. "Although there is something you should know about us," she said at last. "Of course, Deputy Ngonda would be outraged if he knew that we're telling you, but then he finds outrage everywhere." She stooped to his level so that they were face to face. "I rarely think all by myself, Spur." He tried not to notice that her knees bent in different directions. "Most of the time, we think for me."

The world seemed to tilt a little more then; Spur felt as if he might slide off it. "I don't think I understand what you just said."

"It's complicated." She straightened. "And we're attracting attention here. I can hear several young women whispering about us. We should find a more private place to talk. I need your advice." She turned and waved to the citizens in the bleachers who were watching them. Spur forced a smile and waved as well, and then led her up the hill toward town hall.

"Ngonda will file his protest," she said, "and it'll be summarily rejected. We've been in continuous contact with the Forum of the Thousand Worlds." Her speech became choppy as she walked. "They know what we're doing." Climbing the gentle hill left her breathless. "Not all worlds approve. Consensus is hard to come by. But the L'ung have a plan ... to open talks between you ... and the pukpuks." She rested a hand on his shoulder to support herself. "Is that something you think worth doing?"

"Maybe." He could feel the warmth of her hand through the thin fabric of his shirt. "All right, yes." He thought this must be another ploy. "But who are you? Who are the L'ung? Why are you doing this?"

"Be patient." At the top of the hill she had to rest to catch her breath. Finally she said, "You spoke with the High Gregory about gosdogs?"

"In the truck this morning."

"It was at the instigation of the L'ung. Understand that we don't believe that gosdogs think in any meaningful sense of the word. Perhaps the original Peekay intelligence rating was accurate. But if they were found to be more intelligent, then we could bring the issue of their treatment here to the Forum. It would require a delicate touch to steer the debate toward the remedy the L'ung want. Tricky but not impossible. The Forum has no real power to intervene in the affairs of member worlds and your Chairman Winter has the right to run Walden as he pleases. But he depends on the good opinion of the Thousand Worlds. When we're finished here, the L'ung will propose to return the gosdogs to a preserve where they can live in their natural state."

"But there is no natural habitat left. The pukpuks destroyed it."

"Ah, but ecologies can be re-created." She gestured at the lawn stretching before them, at the rose hedges along its border and the trees that shaded it, their leaves trembling in the summer breeze. "As you well know."

"But what does a gosdog preserve have to do with the puk-puks?"

"Come away from the sun before we melt." Memsen led him to a bench in the shadow of an elm. She sagged onto it; Spur remained standing, looking down at her for a change. It eased the crick in his neck.

"The preserve sets a precedent." She clicked her rings. "In order for it to be established, the growth of the forest must be controlled, which means the Transcendent State will be blocked from spreading across Walden. Up until now, the Cooperative has refused to negotiate on this point. And then comes the question of where to put the preserve. You and the pukpuks will have to sit down to decide on a site. Together. With some delicate nudging from the Forum, there's no telling what conversations might take place at such a meeting."

"But we can't!" Spur wiped the sweat from his forehead. "The Transcendent State was founded so that humans could live apart and stay true to ourselves. As long as the pukpuks live here, we'll be under direct attack from upsider ways."

"Your Transcendent State is a controversial experiment." Memsen's face went slack and she made the pa-pa-pa-ptt sound Spur had heard before. "We've always wondered how isolation and ignorance can be suitable foundations for a human society. Do you really believe in simplicity, Spur, or do you just not know any better?"

Spur wondered if she had used some forbidden upsider tech to look into his soul; he felt violated. "I believe in this."

He gestured, as she had done, at Littleton Commons, green as a dream. "I don't want my village to be swept away. The pukpuks destroyed this world once already."

"Yes, that could happen, if it's what you and your children decide," said Memsen. "We don't have an answer for you, Spur. But the question is, do you need a preserve like gosdogs, or are you strong enough to hold onto your beliefs no matter who challenges them?"

"And this is your plan to save Walden?" He ground his shoe into the grass. "This is the luck that the High Gregory came all this way to make?"

"Is it?" She leaned back against the bench and gazed up into the canopy of the elm. "Maybe it is."

"I've been such an idiot." He was bitter; if she was going to use him, at least she could admit it. "You and the High Gregory and the L'ung flit around the upside, having grand adventures and straightening up other people's messes." He began to pace back and forth in front of the bench. "You're like some kind of superheroes, is that it?"

"The L'ung have gathered together to learn statecraft from one another," she said patiently. "Sometimes they travel, but mostly they stay with us on Kenning. Of course they have political power in the Forum because of who they are, but their purpose is not so much to do as it is to learn. Then, in a few more years, this cohort will disband and scatter to their respective worlds to try their luck. And when the time comes for us to marry...."

"Marry? Marry who?"

"The High Gregory, of course."

"But he's just a boy."

Memsen must have heard the dismay in his voice. "He will grow into his own luck soon enough," she said coldly. "I was chosen the twenty-second Memsen by my predecessor. She searched for me for years across the Thousand Worlds." With a weary groan she stood, and once again towered over him. "A Memsen is twice honored: to be wife to one High Gregory and mother to another." Her voice took on a declaiming quality, as if she were giving a speech that had been well rehearsed. "And I carry my predecessor and twenty souls who came before her saved in our memory, so that we may always serve the High Gregory and advise the L'ung."

Spur was horrified at the depth of his misunderstanding of this woman. "You have dead people ... inside you?"

"Not dead," she said. "Saved."

A crazed honking interrupted them. A truck careened around the corner and skidded to a stop in front of the town hall. Stark Sukulgunda flung himself out of the still-running truck and dashed inside.

Spur stood. "Something's wrong." He started for the truck and had gotten as far as the statue of Chairman Winter, high on his pedestal, when Stark burst out of the doors again. He saw Spur and waved frantically.

"Where are they all?" he cried. "Nobody answers."

"Playing baseball." Spur broke into a trot. "What's wrong? What?"

"Baseball?" Stark's eyes bulged as he tried to catch his breath. "South slope of Lamana ... burning ... everything's burning ... the forest is on fire!"

✿ Fourteen

I walked slowly through the wood to Fairhaven cliff, climbed to the highest rock and sat down upon it to observe the progress of the flames, which were rapidly approaching me now about a mile distant from the spot where the fire was kindled. Presently I heard the sound of the distant Bell giving the alarm, and I knew that the town was on its way to the scene. Hitherto I felt like a guilty person. Nothing but shame and regret, but now I settled the matter with myself shortly, and said to myself. Who are these men who are said to be owners of these woods and how am I related to them? I have set fire to the forest, but I have done no wrong therein, and now it is as if the lightning had done it. These flames are but consuming their natural food. So shortly I settled it with myself and stood to watch the approaching flames. It was a glorious spectacle, and I was the only one there to enjoy it. The fire now reached the base of the cliffs and then rushed up its sides. The squirrels ran before it in blind haste, and the pigeons dashed into the midst of the smoke. The flames flashed up the pines to their tops as if they were powder.

    — JOURNAL, 1850

More than half of the Littleton Volunteer Fire Department were playing baseball when the alarm came. They scrambled up the hill to the brick firehouse on the Commons, followed by almost all of the spectators, who crowded anxiously into the communion hall while the firefighters huddled. Normally there would have been sixteen volunteers on call, but, like Spur, Will Sambusa, Bright Ayoub, Bliss Bandaran and Chief Cary Millisap had joined the Corps. Cape was currently Assistant Chief; he would have led the volunteers had not his son been home. Even though Spur protested that he was merely a grunt smokechaser, the volunteers' first act was to vote him Acting Chief.

Like any small-town unit, the Littleton Fire Department routinely answered calls for house fires and brush fires and accidents of all sorts, but they were ill-equipped to stop a major burn. They had just one fire truck, an old quad with a 3,000-liter-per-minute pump and 5,000-liter water tank. It carried fifty meters of six-centimeter hose, fifty meters of booster hose, and a ten-meter mechanical ladder. If the burn was as big as Stark described, Engine No. 4 would be about as much use fighting it as a broom.

Spur resisted the impulse to put his team on the truck and rush out to the burn. He needed more information before he committed his meager forces. It would be at least an hour before companies from neighboring villages would arrive and the Corps might not get to Littleton until nightfall. Cape spread a map out on the long table in the firehouse and the volunteers stood around it, hunch-shouldered and grim. Gandy Joy glided in, lit a single communion square and slipped out again as they contemplated what the burn might do to their village. They took turns peppering Stark with questions about what he had actually seen. At first he tried his best to answer, but he'd had a shock that had knocked better men than him off center. As they pressed him, he grew sullen and suspicious.

The Sukulgundas lived well west of the Leungs and higher up the slope of Lamana Ridge. They'd been latecomers to Littleton and parts of their farmstead were so steep that the fields had to be terraced. They were about four kilometers north of the Commons at the very end of January Road, a steep dirt track with switchbacks. Stark maintained that the burn had come down the ridge at him, from the general direction of Lookover Point to the east. At first he claimed it was maybe a kilometer away when he'd left his place, but then changed his mind and insisted that the burn was practically eating his barn. That didn't make sense, since the strong easterly breeze would push the burn in the opposite direction, toward the farmsteads of the Ezzats and Millisaps and eventually to the Herreras and the Leungs.

Spur shivered as he imagined the burn roaring through GiGa's orchards. But his neighbors were counting on him to keep those fears at bay. "If what you're saying is true," he mused, "it might mean that this fire was deliberately set and that someone is still out there trying to make trouble for us."

"Torches in Littleton?" Livy Jayawardena looked dubious. "We're nowhere near the barrens."

"Neither was Double Down," said Cape. "Or Wheelwright."

"I don't know about that." Stark Sukulgunda pulled the cap off his head and started twisting it. "All I know is that we ought to stop talking about what to do and do something."

"First we have to know for sure where the burn is headed, which means we need to get up the Lamana Ridge Road." Spur was struggling to apply what he'd learned in training. "If the burn hasn't jumped the road and headed back down the north slope of the ridge, then we can use the road as a firebreak and hold that line. And when reinforcements come, we'll send them east over the ridge to the head of the burn. That's the way the wind is blowing everything." He glanced up at the others to see if they agreed. "We need to be thinking hard about an eastern perimeter."

"Why?" Stark was livid. "Because that's where you live? It's my house that—"

"Shut up, Stark," said Peace Toba. "Fill your snoot with communion and get right with the village for a change."

None of the threatened farmsteads that lay in the path of the burn to the east was completely cleared of trees. Simplicity demanded that citizens only cultivate as much of their land as they needed. Farmers across Walden used the forest as a windbreak; keeping unused land in trees prevented soil erosion. But now Spur was thinking about all the pine and hemlock and red cedar, needles laden with resins and oils, side by side with the deciduous trees in the woods where he had played as a boy. At Motu River he'd seen pine trees explode into flame. And then there were the burn piles of slash and stumps and old lumber that every farmer collected, baking in the summer sun.

"If things go wrong in the east, we might need to set our

firebreak as far back as Blue Valley Road." Spur ran his finger down the line on the map. "It won't be as effective a break as the ridge road but we can improve it. Get the Bandarans and Sawatdees to rake off all the forest litter and duff on the west side. Then disk harrow the entire road. I want to see at least a three-meter-wide strip of fresh soil down the entire length."

"Prosper." Cape's voice was hushed. "You're not giving up on all of this." He traced the outline of the four threatened farms on the map, ending on the black square that marked Diligence Cottage.

Spur glanced briefly at his father, then away again, troubled by what he had seen. Capability Leung looked just as desperate as Stark Sukulgunda. Maybe more so, if he thought he had just heard his son pronounce doom on his life's work. For the first time in his life, Spur felt as if he were the father and Cape was the son.

"No." He tried to reassure his father with a smile. "That's just our fall back. What I'm hoping is that we can cut a handline from Spot Pond along Mercy's Creek all the way down to the river. It's rough country and depending on how fast the burn is moving we may not have enough time, but if we can hold that line, we save the Millisaps, Joerlys and us." Left unsaid was that the Ezzats' farmstead would be lost, even if this dicey strategy worked.

"But right now the fire is much closer to my place than anyone else's," said Stark. "And you said yourself, there may be some suicidal maniac just waiting to burn himself up and take my house with him."

Spur was annoyed at the way that Stark Sukulgunda kept buzzing at him. He was making it hard for Spur to concentrate. "We could send the fire truck your way, Stark," he said, "but I don't know what good it would do. You don't have any standing water on your land, do you?"

"Why?"

"The truck only has a 5,000-liter water tank. That's not near enough if your house gets involved."

"We could drop the hard suction line into his well," said Livy. "Pump from there."

"You have a dug well?" said Cape. "How deep?"

"Four meters."

"We'd probably suck it dry before we could do you much good," said Cape.

"No," said Spur. "He's right. Peace, you and Tenny and Cert take No. 4 up to Sukulgundas. You can also establish our western perimeter. Clear a meter-wide handline as far up the ridge as you can. Watch for torches. I don't think the fire is going to come your way but if it does, be ready, understand? Get on the tell and let us know if anything changes."

"We'll call in when we get there," said Peace as her team scattered to collect gear.

"Livy, you and the others round up as many as you can to help with the creek line. We may want to start a backfire, so keep in touch with me on the hand-tell. How much liquid fire have you got?"

"At least twenty grenades. Maybe more. No firebombs though."

"Bring gas then, you'll probably need it. Keep your people between the civilians and the burn, understand? And pull back if it gets too hot. I've lost too many friends this year. I don't want to be burying anyone else. DiDa, you and I need to find a way to get up the ridge ..."

He was interrupted by the roar of a crowd, which had gathered just outside the firehouse. Spur froze, momentarily bewildered. They couldn't still be playing baseball, could they? Then he thought that the burn must have changed direction. It had careened down the ridge faster than it had any right to, an avalanche of fire that was about to incinerate the Commons and there was nothing he could do to fight it; in the nightmare, he wasn't wearing his splash pack. Or his fireproof field jacket. Spur shuddered. He wasn't fit to lead, to decide what to let burn and what to save. He was weak and his soul was lost in darkness and he knew he shouldn't be afraid. He was a veteran of the firefight, but fear squeezed him nonetheless. "Are you all right, son?" His father rested a hand on his shoulder. The burn licked at boulders and scorched the trees in the forest he had sworn to protect.

"DiDa," he whispered, leaning close to his father so no one else would hear, "what if I can't stop it?"

"You'll do your best, Prosper," he said. "Everyone knows that."

As they rushed out of the firehouse, they could see smoke roiling into the sky to the northwest. But the evil plume wasn't what had stunned the crowd, which was still pouring out of the communion hall. A shadow passed directly overhead and, even in the heat of this disastrous afternoon, Spur was chilled.

Silently, like a miracle, the High Gregory's hover landed on Littleton Commons.

✺ Fifteen

Men go to a fire for entertainment. When I see how eagerly men will run to a fire, whether in warm or cold weather, by night or by day, dragging an engine at their heels, I'm astonished to perceive how good a purpose the level of excitement is made to serve.
– JOURNAL, 1850

"There's a big difference between surface fire and crown fire," said the Pendragon Chromlis Furcifer to the L'ung assembled in the belly of the hover. "Surface fires move along the forest floor, burning through the understory." She was reading from notes that scrolled down her forearm.

"Wait, what's understory again?" asked Her Grace, Jacqueline Kristof, who was the youngest of the L'ung.

Memsen pinched the air. "You mustn't keep interrupting, Your Grace. If you have questions, query the cognisphere in slow time." She nodded at Penny. "Go ahead, Pendragon. You're doing a fine job."

"Understory is the grass, shrubs, dead leaves, fallen trees — that stuff. So anyway, a surface fire can burn fast or slow, depending. But if the flames climb into the crowns of the trees, it almost always rips right through the forest. Since the

Transcendental State doesn't have the tech to stop it, Spur will have to let it burn itself out. If you look over there...." The group closed around her, craning to see.

Spur had been able to ignore Penny for the most part, although Cape kept scowling at the L'ung. Memsen had explained that Penny's research topic for the trip to Walden was forest fires.

The hover was not completely proof against smoke. As they skirted the roiling convection column of smoke and burning embers, the air inside the hover became tinged with the bitter stench of the burn. This impressed the L'ung. As they wandered from view to view, they would call to one another. "Here, over here. Do you smell it now? Much stronger over here!"

They had dissolved the partitions and made most of the hull transparent to observe developments in the burn. Just a single three-meter-wide band ran solid from the front of the deck to the back as a concession to Spur and Cape; the L'ung seemed totally immune from fear of heights. Spur was proud at how Cape was handling his first flight in a hover, especially since he himself felt slightly queasy whenever he looked straight down through the deck at the ridge 1,500 meters below.

From this vantage, Spur could see exactly what was needed to contain the burn and realized that he didn't have the resources to do it. Looking to the north, he was relieved that the burn hadn't yet crossed Lamana Ridge Road into the wilderness on the far slope. Barring an unforeseen wind change or embers lighting new spot fires, he thought he might be able to keep the burn within the Littleton valley. But he needed dozens of trained firefighters up on the ridge to defend the road as soon as possible. To the west, he saw where the flames had come close to the Sukulgundas' farmstead, but now the burn there looked to be nothing more than a surface fire that was already beginning to gutter out. Peace and the team with Engine No. 4 should have no trouble mopping up. Then he'd move them onto the ridge, not that just three people and one ancient pumper were going to be enough to beat back a wall of flame two kilometers wide.

"Where you see the darker splotches in the forest, those are evergreens, the best fuel of all," said Penny. "If they catch, you can get a blowup fire, which is what that huge column of smoke is about."

To the east and south, the prospects were grim. The burn had dropped much farther down the ridge than Spur had expected. He remembered from his training that burns were supposed to track uphill faster than down, but the spread to the north and south, upslope and down, looked about the same. As soon as the first crews responded from nearby Bode Well and Highbridge, they'd have to deploy at the base of the ridge to protect the Commons and the farmsteads beyond it.

The head of the burn was a violent crown fire racing east, beneath a chimney of malign smoke that towered kilometers above the hover. When Spur had given the Ezzats and Millisaps permission to save as much as they could from their houses, he'd thought that they'd all have more time. Now he realized that he'd miscalculated. He reached both families using the hand-tell and told them to leave immediately. Bash Ezzat was weeping when she said she could already see the burn sweeping down on her. Spur tried Comfort's tell again to let her know that her farmstead was directly in the path of the burn, but still got no answer.

"DiDa," said Spur gently. He'd been dreading this moment, ever since he'd understood the true scope and direction of the burn. "I think we need to pull Livy and her people back from the creek to Blue Valley Road." He steeled himself against anger, grief and reproach. "There's no time to clear a line," he went on. "At least not one that will stop this burn."

"I think you're right," Cape said, as casually as if they were discussing which trees to prune. "It's simple, isn't it?"

Relieved but still anguished, he hugged his father. "I'm sorry, DiDa." He couldn't remember the last time they had been this close, and was not surprised that Cape did not return his embrace. "Should we send someone to the house?" he said, as he let his father go. "Have them pack some things? Papers, furniture — there's still a little time."

"No." Cape turned and cupped his hands against the transparent hull of the hover. "If I did something silly like that, the farm would burn for sure." He lowered his face into his hands as if to shade the view from glare. But the afternoon sun was a dim memory, blotted out by the seething clouds of smoke.

Spur shut his eyes then, so tight that for a moment he

could feel muscles on his temple quiver. "Memsen," he said, his voice catching in his throat, "can you put us down by the Sawatdees' house?"

Spur got more resistance from Livy than he had from his father. It took him almost ten minutes to convince her that trying to dig a firebreak along Mercy's Creek was not only futile but also dangerous. When it was over, he felt drained. As he flopped beside Cape onto one of the chairs that Memsen had caused to flow from the deck of the hover, the hand-tell squawked. He groaned, anticipating that Livy was back with a new argument.

"Prosper Leung?" said a woman's voice.

"Speaking."

"I'm Commander Do Adoula, Fourth Engineers. My squad was on CR in Longwalk but we heard you have a situation there and we're on our way. We can be in Littleton in half an hour. I understand you're in a hover. What do you see?"

The handover of command was subtle but swift. Commander Adoula started by asking questions and ended by giving orders. She was coming in four light trucks with thirty-seven firefighters but no heavy equipment. She approved of Spur's decision to stop the burn at Blue Valley Road, and split her force in two while they were speaking, diverting half to the ridge and half to help Livy on Blue Valley. She directed the local firefighters from Bode Well and Highbridge to dig in on the south to protect the Commons and requested that Spur stay in the hover and be her eyes in the sky.

When they finished talking, Spur slumped back against his chair. He was pleased that Adoula had ratified his firefighting plans, relieved to be no longer in charge.

"The Corps?" said Cape.

"Fourth Engineers." He folded the hand-tell. "They were on CR in Longwalk."

"That was lucky."

"Lucky," he agreed. He spotted the High Gregory whispering to Memsen. "How are you doing, DiDa?"

"You know, I've never visited the ocean." Cape blinked as he stared through the hull at the forest below. "Your mother wanted me to take her there, did I ever tell you that?"

"No."

"She always used to ask if we owned the farm or if the farm owned us." He made a low sound, part sigh and part whistle. "I wonder if she's still in Providence."

Spur didn't know what to say.

Cape frowned. "You haven't been in contact with her?"

"No."

"If you ever do speak to her, would you tell me?"

"Sure."

He nodded and made the whistling sound again.

"A burn this big is different from a surface fire," said Penny. "It's so hot that it makes a kind of fire weather called a convection column. Inside the column, bubbles of super-heated air are surging up, only we can't see that. But on the outside, the cooler smoky edges are pouring back toward the ground."

"Yes, yes." The High Gregory pointed, clearly excited. "Watch at the top, to the left of the plume. It's like it's turning itself inside out."

"Awesome," said Kai Thousandfold. "Do you remember those gas sculptures we played with on Blimminey?"

"But that's going to be a problem for Spur and his firefighters," said Penny. "It's like a chimney shooting sparks and embers high into the atmosphere. They might come down anywhere and start new fires."

"Is anyone going to die?" said Senator Dowm.

"We hope not," Memsen said. "Spur is doing his best and help is on the way."

"Don't you wish she'd shut up?" muttered Cape, leaning into Spur. "This isn't some silly class. They're watching our life burn down."

"They're from the upside, DiDa. We can't judge them."

"And how does she know so much about how we fight fires? Look at her, she's just a kid."

That had been bothering Spur too, and it was getting harder and harder to put out of his mind. When had the L'ung had time to do all this research? They had arrived the day after he had first spoken to the High Gregory. Had they known ahead of time that they were coming to Walden? Was all this part of the plan?

"Memsen says they're special," he said.

"Spur." The High Gregory signed for him to come over. "Come take a look at this."

He crossed the deck to where the L'ung were gathered. The

hover had descended to a thousand meters and was cruising over the Joerly farmstead.

"There," said the High Gregory, pointing to the woods they had tramped through that morning, a mix of hard and softwoods: birch and oak, hemlock and pine. In the midst of it, three tendrils of gray smoke were climbing into the sky.

"Those are spot fires," said Penny. "Caused by falling embers."

Spur didn't believe it. He'd been worried about spotting all along and had swung from side to side in the hover looking for them. But he'd decided that not enough time had passed for embers from the burn to start raining down on them. The convection column towered at least five kilometers above the valley. He stared at the plumes of smoke rising from the woods of his childhood with sickening dread. From right to left they were progressively smaller. Three fires in a series, which meant they had probably been set. What was his duty here? He was pretty sure that his scooter was still in the barn at Diligence Cottage. He could use it to get away from the burn in plenty of time. Cape could monitor the progress of the burn for Commander Adoula. Besides, if someone was down there setting fires....

Someone.

"Memsen," he said. "I've changed my mind."

The hover glided to a stop above the unused field nearest to Diligence Cottage. Spur stepped back as guard rails flowed out of the deck around the ramp, which slowly extended like a metal tongue toward the sweet clover below. Cape, who was standing next to Spur, was smiling. What did his father think was so funny?

"We can stay here and wait for you," said Memsen. "If you have a problem, we'll come."

"Not through those trees you won't," said Spur, "No, you take Cape back up so he can report to the commander." The hover shuddered in the windstorm caused by the burn. "Besides, it's going to get rough here before too much longer. You need to protect yourselves."

"This is exciting." Her Grace, Jacqueline Kristof clapped her hands. "Are you excited, Spur?"

Memsen turned the girl around and gave her a hard shove toward the rest of the L'ung.

"DiDa?" Spur wanted to hug his father but settled for handing him the tell. "When the commander calls, just explain that I think we might have a torch and I'm on the ground looking. Then just keep track of the burn for her."

"Yes." His father was grinning broadly now. "I'm ready."

"Good. Memsen, thanks for your help."

"Go safely." She clicked her rings.

Spur held out his hand to the High Gregory but the boy dodged past it and embraced him instead. Spur was taken aback when he felt the High Gregory's kiss on his cheek. "I can see much more luck for you, friend Spur," he murmured. "Don't waste it."

The hot wind was an immediate shock after the cool interior of the hover. It blew gusty and confused, whipping

Spur's hair and picking at his short sleeves. Spur paused at the bottom of the ramp to consider his next move and gather his courage. The pillar of smoke had smothered the afternoon sun, sinking the land into nightmarish and untimely gray twilight.

"Nice weather we're having," said Cape.

"DiDa, what?" He spun around, horrified. "Get back up there."

Cape snapped him a mock salute. "Since when do you give the orders on this farm, son?"

"But you have to, you can't...." He felt like a foolish little boy, caught by his father pretending to be a grownup. "Someone has to talk to the ground. The commander needs to know what's happening with the burn."

"I gave the tell to your know-so-much friend, Penny. She'll talk Adoula's ear off."

The ramp started to retract.

"What I have to do is too dangerous, DiDa." Spur's face was hot. "You're not coming, understand?"

"Wasn't planning to." Cape chuckled. "Never entered my mind."

Spur watched in helpless fury as the hatch closed. "Then just load whatever you want into the truck and take off. You've got maybe twenty minutes before things get hot here."

The hover rose straight up and away from the field but then paused, a dark speck in an angry sky.

"See what you've done?" Spur groaned.

"Don't worry. They'll run before too long." Cape clapped

him on the back. "I don't know about you, but I have things to do."

"DiDa, are you...?" Spur was uncertain whether he should leave Cape while he was in this manic mood. "Be careful."

Capability Roger Leung was not a man known for his sense of humor, but he laughed now. "Prosper, if we were being careful, we'd be up there in the sky with your strange little friends." He pointed into the woods. "Time to take some chances, son."

He turned and trotted off toward the big house without looking back.

Spur knew these woods. He and Vic and Comfort had spent hours in the cool shade pretending to be pirates or skantlings or aliens or fairies. They played queen and castle in the pukpuk ruins and pretended to be members of Morobe's original crew, exploring a strange new world for the first time. They cut paths to secret hideouts and built lean-tos from hemlock boughs and, when Vic and Spur were eleven, they even erected a ramshackle tree house with walls and a roof, although Cape made them take it down because he said it was too dangerous. Spur had been kissed for the first time in that tree house: In a contest of sibling gross out, Vic had dared his big sister to kiss his best friend. Comfort got the best of it, however, because her back dare was that Vic had to kiss Spur. As he pulled back from the kiss, Vic had punched Spur in the arm so hard it left a bruise.

The woods were dark and unnaturally quiet as he padded

down the path that led past Bear Rock and the Throne of the Spruce King. Spur heard no birdsong or drone of bugs. It was as if the trees themselves were listening for the crackle of fire. When he first smelled smoke, he stopped to turn slowly and sniff, trying to estimate where it had come from. Ahead and to the north was his best guess. That meant it was time to cut off the path and bushwhack south across the Great Gosdog Swamp, which had never been very great and always dried up in the summer. His plan was to strike out in the direction of the smallest of the three fires he had seen from the hover. He knew he was getting close when it started to snow fire.

Most of what floated down was ash, but in the mix were sparks and burning embers that stung the bare skin of his arms and face. He brushed a hand through his hair and ran. Not in a panic — just to keep embers from sticking to him. To his right he could see the glow of at least one of the fires. And yes, now he could hear the distant crack and whoosh he knew all too well. The burn was working along the forest floor, he was sure of that. Crown fire sounded like a runaway train. If he were anywhere near one, he'd be deafened and then he'd be dead. Spur finally escaped the ash fall after several minutes of dodging past trees at speed. He hunched over to knead the stitch in his side, then pressed on.

The wind had picked up and now was blowing west, not east. He thought it must be an indraft. The burn that was crashing down on them had to suck air in huge gulps from every direction in order to support itself. Maybe the wind shift would work in their favor. A west wind would push these outlying spot fires back toward the burn itself. If the line of backfire was wide enough, it might actually check the advance of the burn when the two met. Of course, it would have to scorch across the best parts of the Millisap and Joerly farmsteads first.

In the gathering darkness, Spur decided to start trotting again. It was taking too long to skirt around the last fire to Mercy's Creek. And unless he saw something soon, he was turning back. He had to leave himself enough time to get away. And he wanted to make sure his father hadn't done anything crazy.

Intent on not tripping over a stone or root, Spur never saw the windblown curtain of smoke until it closed around him. He spun around, disoriented. He had been panting from running, so his nose and mouth and lungs filled immediately. It was like trying to breathe cotton. His eyes went teary and the world was reduced to a watery dissolve. Had he been out with Gold Squad, he would have been wearing goggles, a helmet and a breather. But here he was practically naked, and the smoke was pervasive and smothering. He was coughing so hard he could taste the tang of blood and then his throat closed and he knew he was about to choke to death. In a panic, he hurled himself flat against the forest floor, desperately searching for the shallow layer of breathable air that they said sometimes clung to the ground. A stump poked at his side but as he laid his cheek against the mat of twigs and papery leaves, he found cooler air, rank but breathable. He tried to fill his aching lungs, coughed up mucus and blood, then tried again.

Spur didn't know exactly how long he lay there, but when he came to himself again, the haze of smoke had thinned to gauze and he knew he had taken enough chances. He had learned the hard way at Motu River that he was no hero. Why was he at it again? No more; get to the cottage, get on the scooter and get as far away from fire as possible. He pushed himself up on hands and knees, coughed and spat. His nose felt as if someone had pulled barbed wire through it. He sat back on his heels, blinking. It wasn't until he brushed at the leaf litter on his face that he realized he'd been crying. When he finally stood, he felt tottery. He grabbed a sapling to steady himself. Then he heard a twig snap and the rustle of foliage being parted. He ducked behind a beech tree that was barely wider than he was.

Comfort came trudging toward him, her face hard, eyes glassy. One look told him everything. She had changed out of the gingham dress into a pair of baggy work pants that looked like they must have belonged to Vic. Over a smudged and dirty T-shirt, she wore a crude burlap vest to which were attached three liquid-fire grenades. They bumped against her chest as she approached. She looked weary, as if she'd been carrying a weight that had pushed her to the very limit of her strength.

He had thought to leap out and overwhelm her when

she passed, but she spotted him when she was still a dozen meters away, and froze. He stepped from behind his tree, his hands held in front of him.

"I won't hurt you," he said.

In the instant he saw mindless animal panic in her eyes, he thought her more alien than any upsider. He had spooked her. Then she turned and sprinted away.

Spur ran after her. He wasn't thinking about the burn or his village or simplicity. He ran. He didn't have time to be either brave or afraid. He ran because he had loved this woman once and because he had watched her brother die.

As a girl, Comfort had always been the nimblest of the three of them. In an open field, Vic would have caught her, but scooting past trees and ducking under low branches, Comfort was faster than any two squirrels. After a couple of minutes of pursuit, Spur was winded. He wasn't exactly sure where they were anymore. Headed toward the creek, he guessed. If she thought she could cross over and take refuge in her own house, she truly was crazy. Suicidal.

Which made him pick up the pace, despite his fatigue. He ran so hard he thought his heart might break.

She had almost reached the creek when the chase ended abruptly. Comfort got reckless, cut a tree too close and clipped it instead. The impact knocked one of the grenades loose and spun her half around. She went to her knees and Spur leapt at her. But she kicked herself away and he skidded past and crashed into a tangle of summersweet. By the time he got to his knees she was showing him one of the grenades.

He could see that she had flipped the safety and that her finger was on the igniter.

"Stop there," she said.

Spur was breathless and a little dizzy. "Comfort, don't."

"Too late." She blew a strand of dark hair off her face. "I already have."

He stood, once again holding his hands where she could see them. "What's this about, Comfort?"

"Vic," she said. "It's mostly about Vic now."

"He's gone. There's nothing you can do for him."

"We'll see." She shivered, despite the heat. "It was my fault, you know. I was the one who recruited him. But he was just supposed to pass information." Her voice shook. "They must have bullied him into becoming a torch. I killed him, Spur. I killed my brother."

"Listen to me, Comfort. He wasn't a torch. It was an accident."

The hand holding the grenade trembled slightly but then steadied. "That's not what you said this morning when you were off your head." She gave him a pitying look. "You said you tried to save him. That I believe."

He took a half-step toward her. "But how does it help anyone to set fire to Littleton?" Another half-step. "To our farms?"

She backed away from him. "They could stop this, you know. Your upsider friends. They could force the Cooperative to settle, put pressure on Jack Winter to do what's right. Except they don't really care about us. They come to watch, but they never get involved." Her laugh was low and scattered. "They're involved now. I hope that little brat is scared of dying."

"But they do care." He held his arms tight to his sides; otherwise he would have been waving them at her. "Memsen has a plan." Spur thought he might yet save her. "You have to believe me, Comfort. There are going to be talks with the pukpuks."

"Right." Her mouth twisted. "And you didn't see Vic torch himself."

"Besides, did you really think you could burn them up? The High Gregory is safe, Comfort. Memsen and the L'ung. Their hover came for us. That's how I got here so fast. They're in the air," he pointed backward over his shoulder, "waiting for me over the cottage."

When he saw her gaze flick up and away from him, he launched himself. He grabbed at the arm with the grenade. They twirled together in a grotesque pirouette. Then, unable to check his momentum, Spur stumbled and fell.

Comfort stepped away from him. She shook her head once. She pressed the igniter on the grenade.

It exploded into a fireball that shot out two long streams of flame in opposite directions. One soared high into the trees, the other shot down at the forest floor and gathered in a blazing puddle at her feet. She screamed as the grenade fell from her charred hand. Great tongues of flame licked up her legs. Her pants caught fire. Her singed hair curled into nothingness.

Spur screamed too. Seeing it all happen all over again was worse than any nightmare. When Vic had set the liquid firebomb off, he had been instantly engulfed in flame. Spur had tried to knock him down, hoping to roll his friend onto the ground and put the merciless fire out. But Vic had shoved him away. With his clothes, his arms in flames, Vic had found the strength to send Spur sprawling backward.

Which saved Spur's life when the second bomb went off.

But this wasn't Motu River and Vic was dead. Comfort, his Comfort had only grenades, designed to set backfires, not bombs designed by pukpuk terrorists. The lower half of her body had been soaked in liquid fire and was burning but he could see her face, her wild, suffering eyes, her mouth a slash of screeching pain and that last grenade still bumping against her chest.

Spur flew at her and ripped the unexploded grenade from the vest. He swept her up in his arms, taking her weight easily with a mad strength, and raced toward the creek. He had the crazy thought that if he ran fast enough, he would be able to stay ahead of the pain. He knew he was burning now but he had to save her. He had never had a chance with Vic; take some chances, his father had said, and the High Gregory had warned him not to waste his luck. But the pain was too fast, it was catching up to him. Comfort's screams filled his head and then he was flying. He splashed down on top of her in the cool water and she didn't struggle when he forced her under, counting one, two, three, four, five, and he yanked her up and screamed at her to breathe, breathe, and when she choked and gasped, he thrust her down again, two, three, four, five and when he pulled her up again she was limp; his poor burned Comfort had either fainted away or died in his arms but at least she wasn't on fire anymore.

Neither of them was.

✿ Sixteen

The light which puts out our eyes is darkness to us.
Only that day dawns to which we are awake.
— WALDEN

In the dream, Spur sits in the kitchen of Diligence Cottage with Comfort, who is wearing the jade-colored pajamas. There are pies everywhere. Apple and cherry pies are stacked on the counters and across the table. Blackberry, elderberry and blueberry pies are lined up on the new oak floor against the wall with its morning glory wallpaper that Comfort ordered all the way from Providence, which is where Spur's mother lives. Maybe. He should find out. Comfort has set fiesta pear and peach surprise pies on top of the refrigerator and laid out the rhubarb pies two to a chair. Whatever else people in Littleton say about her, everyone agrees that Comfort makes the best pumpkin pies anywhere. In the dream, the pies are her idea. She has made enough pie to last him the rest of his life. He will need it if she goes. In the dream, though, it's not certain that she is leaving and he's not sure he wants her to. Besides, she certainly isn't going to catch the train back to Longwalk in those pajamas. They slide right off when you tug at them, the smooth fabric sliding lightly against her skin. In the dream she threads her way around a strawberry pie so she can kiss him. At first her kiss is like a promise. After a kiss like this, he should kick open the bedroom door and throw back the covers. But the kiss ends like a question. And the answer is no, Spur doesn't want this woman to be unhappy anymore because of him. He doesn't want to dry her tears or....

"Enough sleeping, son." A sharp voice sliced through his dream. "Wake up and join the world."

Spur blinked, then gasped in disappointment. It wasn't fair; he didn't get to keep Comfort or the pie. The strange room he was in seemed to be a huge bay window filled with sunlight. In it was a scatter of dark shapes, one of which was moving. A cold hand pressed against his forehead.

"38.2 degrees," said the docbot. "But then a little fever is to be expected."

"Dr. Niss?" said Spur.

"I'm never happy to see repeat customers, son." The docbot shined pinlights into Spur's eyes. "Do you know where you are? You were a little woozy when we picked you up."

He licked his lips, trying to recall. "The hospital?"

"Allworthy Memsen's hover. Open your mouth and say ahh." The docbot brushed its medfinger across Spur's tongue, leaving a waxy residue that tasted like motor oil.

"The hover?" There was something important that Spur couldn't quite remember. "But how did you get here?"

"I'm on call, son," said the docbot. "I can be anywhere

there's a bot. Although this isn't much of an implementation. Feels two sizes too small."

Spur realized then that this docbot was different from the one at the hospital. It only had two gripper arms and its eye was set on top of its headplate. What did he mean, repeat customers? Then the memory of the burn went roaring through his head. "Comfort!" Spur tried to sit up but the docbot pushed him back down. "Is she all right?"

"Still with us. We've saved her for now. But we'll talk about that after we look at your burns."

"How long have I been here? Did they stop the burn?"

The docbot reached behind Spur's neck, untied the hospital gown and pulled it to his waist. "I kept you down all last night and the better part of today to give your grafts a chance to take." The new set of burns ran in rough stripes across his chest. There was a splotch like a misshapen handprint on top of his shoulder. "You'll be on pain blockers for the next few days — they can poke holes in your memory, so don't worry if you forget how to tie your shoes." The docbot flowed warm dermslix onto the grafts. "Dermal regeneration just 13 percent," it muttered.

"The burn, what about the burn?"

"Your people have it under control, according to that little Pendragon girl. I guess there's still some mopping up to do, but at least those kids are finally settling down. They were bouncing off the walls all last night." He pulled the gown back up. "You'll be fine son. Just stop playing with fire."

Spur was already swinging his legs off the bed as he fumbled with the ties of the gown. But when he went to stand, the deck seemed to fall away beneath his feet.

"Whoops." The docbot caught him. "Another side effect of pain blockers is that they'll tilt your sense of balance." He eased him back onto the bed. "You're going to want someone to help you get around for now. The docbot twisted off its medfinger and dropped it in the sterilizer. "I've got just the party for you. Wait here and I'll send him in."

The docbot had scarcely popped out of the room when the High Gregory came bursting in, pushing a wheelchair. The entire bubble wall collapsed momentarily to reveal the L'ung, who started whooping and applauding for Spur. Memsen slipped in just as the wall reformed.

"You are the craziest, luckiest, bravest person I know." The High Gregory was practically squeaking with excitement. "What were you thinking when you picked her up? We were cheering so loud we thought you could probably hear us down there. I couldn't sleep all night, just thinking about it. Did you hear the L'ung just now? I taught them to clap hands for you. Here, have a seat."

Spur allowed Memsen and the High Gregory to help him into the chair, although he was certain they were going to drop him. He shut his eyes, counted to three and when he opened them again the cabin had stopped chasing its tail. "How do you know what I did?"

"We watched," said Memsen. "From the moment you stepped off the ramp, our spybugs were on you. The High Gregory is right. We were very moved."

"You watched?" He felt his cheeks flush. "I could've been killed."

"Watch is all we're supposed to do," said Memsen, "according to your covenant."

"But Memsen said we couldn't just leave you after you jumped into the water with her," said the High Gregory. "So we mowed down some forest to get to you, pulled the two of you out of the creek and qiced Dr. Niss into a bot that Betty Twosalt made." He wheeled Spur toward the hull so he could see the view. "She's good. She won a prize for her bots once."

"And Comfort is all right?" Spur glanced back over his shoulder at Memsen. "That's what Dr. Niss said."

"Saved," said Memsen, clicking her rings together. "We were able to save her."

The High Gregory parked the wheelchair as near to the hull as he could get, and set the brake. He made the deck transparent too, so they could see more of the valley. "It's huge, Spur," he said, gesturing through the hull at the remains of the burn. "I've never seen anything like it."

They were passing over Mercy's Creek headed for the Joerlys, although he scarcely recognized the land beneath them as he surveyed the damage. The fires Comfort had started must have been sucked by the indraft back toward the burn as Spur had hoped, creating a backfired barrier to its progress. The backfire and the head of the burn must have met somewhere just east of the Joerlys. Comfort's house, barn and all the sheds had burned to their foundations. Farther to the west, the Millisap and Ezzat farmsteads were also obliterated. And more than half of Lamana Ridge was a wasteland of blackened spikes rising out of gray ash. Wisps of white smoke drifted across the ravaged land like the ghosts of dead trees. But dispersed through the devastation were inexplicable clumps of unscathed forest, mostly deciduous hardwood. Spur was relieved to see a blue-green crown of forest to the north along the top of the ridge, where the Corps must have beaten the burn back.

"What about the east?" said Spur. "Where did they stop it?"

But the hover was already turning and his view shifted, first south, where he could see the steeple of the communion hall on the Commons then southeast where CR22 sliced a thin line through intact forest. The High Gregory was watching him, his yellow eyes alight with anticipation.

"What?" said Spur, irked to be putting on a show for this fidgety upsider. "What are you staring at?"

"You," said the High Gregory. "There's so much luck running in your family, Spur. You know we tried to pick your father up after we got you, but he wouldn't come, even though we told him you were hurt."

"He was still there? That old idiot. Is he all right?"

"He's fine." The High Gregory patted Spur's hand. "He said he wasn't going to give his farm up without a fight. He had all your hoses out. He had this great line—I can't remember it exactly." He looked to Memsen for help. "Something about spitting?"

Memsen waited as a bench began to form from the deck. "Your father said that if the pump gave out, he'd spit at the burn until his mouth went dry."

Spur had raised himself out of the wheelchair, craning to see as the farm swung into view. The big house, the barns, the cottage were all untouched. But the orchards. . . .

"He started his own backfire." Spur sank back onto the seat. Over half the trees were gone: the Macintosh and GoReds and Pippins were charred skeletons. But at least Cape had saved the Alumars and the Huangs and the Galas. And GiGo's trees by the cottage, all those foolish Macouns.

"The wind had changed direction." Memsen sat on the bench facing Spur. "When we arrived, he had just knocked a hole in the gas tank of your truck and said he couldn't stop to talk. He was going drive through his orchard and then set the backfire. We thought it seemed dangerous so we put spybugs on him. But he knew exactly what he was about." She showed Spur her teeth. "He's a brave man."

"Yes," mused Spur, although he wondered if that were true. Maybe his father just loved his apples more than he loved his life. Spur felt the hover accelerate then and the ground below began to race by. They shot over the Commons and headed west in the direction of Longwalk.

"We watched all night," said the High Gregory, "just like your father told us. Memsen made Penny let everyone have a turn talking to Commander Adoula on the tell. The fire was so awesome in the dark. We flew through it again and again."

The High Gregory's enthusiasm continued to annoy Spur.

Three farmsteads were gone and his own orchards decimated, but this boy thought he was having an adventure. "You didn't offer to help? You could've dropped splash on the burn, maybe diverted it from the houses."

"We did offer," said Memsen. "We were told that upsiders are allowed to render assistance in the deep forest where only firefighters can see us, but not in plain sight of a village or town."

"Memsen is in trouble for landing the hover on the Commons." The High Gregory settled beside her on the bench. "We haven't even told anyone yet about what we did for you by the creek."

"So." Memsen held out her hand to him, fingers outspread. "We've been called back to Kenning to answer for our actions."

"Really?" Spur felt relieved but also vaguely disappointed. "When will you go?"

"Now, actually." Her rings glittered in the sunlight. "We asked Dr. Niss to wake you so we could say goodbye."

"But who will take Comfort and me to the hospital?"

"We'll be in Longwalk in a few moments. There's a hospital in Benevolence Park Number 2." Her fingers closed into a fist. "But Comfort will be coming with us."

"What?" Despite himself, Spur lurched out of the wheelchair. He tottered, the cabin spun, and the next thing he knew both Memsen and the High Gregory were easing him back down.

"Why?" He took a deep breath. "She can't."

"She can't very well stay in Littleton," said the High Gregory. "Her farm is destroyed. You're going to have to tell everyone who started the burn."

"Am I?" He considered whether he would lie to protect her. After all, he had lied for her brother. "She's told you she wants to do this? Let me talk to her."

"That's not possible." Memsen pinched the air.

"Why not?"

"Do you want to come with us, Spur?" said the High Gregory. "You could, you know."

"No." He wheeled himself backward, horrified at the idea. "Why would I want to do that? My home is in Littleton. I'm a farmer."

"Then stop asking questions," said Memsen impatiently. "As a citizen of the Transcendent State you're under a consensual cultural quarantine. We've just been reminded of that quite forcefully. There's nothing more we can say to you."

"I don't believe this." Spur heard himself shouting. "You've done something to her and you're afraid to tell me. What is it?"

Memsen hesitated, and Spur heard the low, repetitive pa-pa-pa-ptt that he had decided she made when she was consulting her predecessors. "If you insist, we can make it simple for you." Memsen thrust her face close to his. "Comfort died," she said harshly. "Tell that to everyone in your village. She was horribly burned and she died."

Spur recoiled from her. "But you said you saved her. Dr. Niss . . . ."

"Dr. Niss can show you the body, if you care to see it." She straightened. "So."

"Goodbye, Spur," said the High Gregory. "Can we help you back onto the bed?"

Beneath them Spur could see the outskirts of Longwalk. Abruptly the hull of the hover turned opaque and the ceiling of the cabin began to glow. Spur knew from watching hovers land from the window of his hospital room that they camouflaged themselves on the final approach over a city.

"No, wait." Spur was desperate to keep the upsiders talking. "You said she was going with you. I definitely heard that. You said she was saved. Is she . . . this is like the other Memsens that you told me about, isn't it? The ones that are saved in you?"

"This is a totally inappropriate conversation." Memsen pinched the air with both hands. "We'll have to ask Dr. Niss to strike it from your memory."

"He can do that?"

"Sure," said the High Gregory. "We do it all the time. But he has to replace it with some fake memory. You'll have to tell him what you want. And if you should ever come across anything that challenges the replacement memory, you could get . . . ."

Spur held up his hand to silence him. "But it's true what I just said?"

Memsen snorted in disgust and turned to leave.

"She can't admit anything." The High Gregory grasped her hand to restrain her. He held it to his chest. "But yes."

Spur was gripping the push rims of his wheelchair so hard that his hands ached. "So nobody dies on the upside?"

"No, no. Everybody dies. It's just that some of us choose to be saved to a shell afterward. Even the saved admit it's not the same as being alive. I haven't made my mind up about all that yet, but I'm only twelve standard. My birthday is next week, I wish you could be there."

"What will happen to Comfort in this shell?"

"She's going to have to adjust. She didn't expect to be saved, of course, probably didn't even know it was possible, so when they activate her, she'll be disoriented. She'll need some kind of counseling. We have some pretty good soulmasons on Kenning. And they can send for her brother; he'll want to help."

"Stop it! This is cruel." Memsen yanked his hand down. "We have to go right now."

"Why?" said the High Gregory plaintively. "He's not going to remember any of this."

"Vic was saved?" Even though he was still safe in the wheelchair, he felt as if he were falling.

"All the pukpuk martyrs were." The High Gregory tried to shake his hand loose from Memsen, but she wouldn't let him go. "That was why they agreed to sacrifice themselves."

"Enough." Memsen started to drag him from the cabin. "We're sorry, Spur. You're a decent man. Go back to your cottage and your apples and forget about us."

"Goodbye, Spur," called the High Gregory as they popped through the bulkhead. "Good luck."

As the bulkhead shivered with their passing, he felt a fierce and troubling desire burn his soul. Some part of him did want to go with them, to be with Comfort and Vic on the upside and see the wonders that Chairman Winter had forbidden the citizens of the Transcendent State. He could do it; he knew he could. After all, everyone in Littleton seemed to think he was leaving.

But then who would help Cape bring in the harvest?

Spur wasn't sure how long he sat alone in the wheelchair with a thousand thoughts buzzing in his head. The upsiders had just blown up his world and he was trying desperately to piece it back together. Except what was the point? In a little while he wasn't going to be worrying anymore about Comfort and Vic and shells and being saved. Maybe that was for the best; it was all too complicated. Just like the Chairman had said. Spur thought he'd be happier thinking about apples and baseball and maybe kissing Melody Velez. He was ready to forget.

He realized that the hover had gone completely still. There was no vibration from the hull skimming through the air, no muffled laughter from the L'ung. He watched the hospital equipment melt into the deck. Then all the bulkheads popped and he could see the entire bay of the hover. It was empty except for his wheelchair, a gurney with Comfort's shroud-covered body and the docbot, which rolled up to him.

"So you're going to make me forget all this?" said Spur bitterly. "All the secrets of the upside?"

"If that's what you want."

Spur shivered. "I have a choice?"

"I'm just the doctor, son. I can offer treatment but you have to accept it. For example, you chose not to tell me how you got burned that first time." The docbot rolled behind the wheelchair. "That pretty much wrecked everything I was trying to accomplish with the conciliation sim."

Spur turned around to look at it. "You knew all along?"

The docbot locked into the back of the wheelchair. "I wouldn't be much of a doctor if I couldn't tell when patients were lying to me." It started pushing Spur toward the hatch.

"But you work for the Chairman." Spur didn't know if he wanted the responsibility for making this decision.

"I take Jack Winter's money," said the docbot. "I don't take his advice when it comes to medical or spiritual practice."

"But what if I tell people that Comfort and Vic are saved and that upsiders get to go on after they die?"

"Then they'll know."

Spur tried to imagine keeping the upsiders' immortality a secret for the rest of his days. He tried to imagine what would happen to the Transcendent State if he told what he knew. His mouth went as dry as flour. He was just a farmer, he told himself; he didn't have that good an imagination. "You're saying that I don't have to have my memory of all this erased?"

"Goodness, no. Unless you'd rather forget about me."

As they passed Comfort's body, Spur said, "Stop a minute."

He reached out and touched the shroud. He expected it to be some strange upsider fabric but it was just a simple cotton sheet. "They knew that I could choose to remember, didn't they? Memsen and the High Gregory were playing me to the very end."

"Son," said Dr. Niss, "the High Gregory is just a boy and nobody in the Thousand Worlds knows what the Allworthy knows."

But Spur had stopped listening. He rubbed the shroud between his thumb and forefinger, thinking about how he and the Joerlys used to make up adventures in the ruins along Mercy's Creek when they were children. Often as not one of them would achieve some glorious death as part of the game. The explorer would boldly drink from the poisoned cup to free her comrades, the pirate captain would be run through defending his treasure, the queen of skantlings would throw down her heartstone rather than betray the castle. And then he or Vic or Comfort would stumble dramatically to the forest floor and sprawl there, cheek pressed against leaf litter, as still as scattered stones. The others would pause briefly over the body and then dash into the woods, so that the fallen hero could be reincarnated and the game could go on.

"I want to go home," he said, at last. ✸